I0596482

Below the Trestle

Allen Sircy

Copyright © 2025 Allen Sircy

All rights reserved. No part of this publication may be reproduced, distributed, or transmitted in any form or by any means, including photocopying, recording, or other electronic or mechanical methods, without the prior written permission of the publisher, except in the case of brief quotations embodied in critical reviews and certain other noncommercial uses permitted by copyright law.

Published by Southern Ghost Stories, Gallatin, Tennessee

ISBN: 979-8-9988146-4-8

Table of Contents

Prologue 4

The Crossing 6

I Got a Knife 10

Bodies... 16

Banana Nut 29

World of Wonders.. 36

The World's Tallest Man 42

The Police Car in the Driveway 59

Ashes to Ashes.. 68

GOATMAN LIVES?.. 73

Livestream 77

"Start from the Beginning 85

Contact... 91

"Momma's Here" 103

Goatman Fever 118

A Hive of Chaos 125

Manhunt.. 135

The Trestle.. 137

Beloved Son.. 140

Southbound... 150

Downstream.. 157

Epilogue... 159

Prologue

They called him the Goatman.

For generations, whispers spread around Louisville, Kentucky about some kind of a creature near Pope Lick Creek that threw people off of a train trestle. Some swore it was a circus freak that escaped a train wreck long ago, half-man, half-beast, condemned to wander the woods. Others claimed he was the Devil's offspring, born of some unholy union, luring the curious to their deaths on the rails. Still more insisted it was nothing but a story—an old Kentucky scare-tale told to keep children from trespassing near the deadly train trestle.

But stories have power, especially in a place where tragedy clings like moss to stone. The trestle had claimed dozens of lives over the years—daredevils chasing the thrill of the legend, lovers daring each other to climb, drifters who miscalculated the distance between steel and earth. Each time a body was pulled from the creek, the tale grew darker, more certain. People stopped asking *if* the Goatman was real. They only asked *when* he would appear again.

They said if you went to the trestle at night, you might hear the low bleat of a goat where no goat should be. You might see eyes gleaming from the tree line, or catch the shadow of horns against the moonlit sky. The lucky ones ran before they saw more. The unlucky never came back at all.

And yet, despite every warning, people kept coming. They always do. Something about the trestle draws them still—the thrill-seekers, the curious, the ones who want to laugh at an old story. They come thinking it's just a legend. They leave—if they leave—never laughing again.

Because the Goatman, whatever he truly is, waits in those woods. Patient. Watching.

And he has never forgotten the sound of blood hitting the rocks.

The Crossing

On a crisp October afternoon in 2018, the freight train roared like a living beast, its horn shrieking as it thundered down the rural Kentucky tracks. The rails shimmered with vibration. Red lights blinked on the crossbuck at the empty crossing, but there were no gates—no mechanical arms to bar the road, just a lonely warning flashing in the fall daylight.

From a distance, the engine of a yellow 1995 Mustang howled in reply, eating up the asphalt as it tore down the country road. Behind the wheel sat John Summers, nineteen and bulletproof, his hair catching the wind like a banner of rebellion. A cigarette clung to the corner of his mouth, trembling with the force of the speed. Metallica's "No Leaf Clover" blared from the speakers—his own personal soundtrack to chaos.

John didn't flinch. He grinned.

The Mustang's engine screamed as he gunned it. The car bolted forward, surging through the crossing just heartbeats before the train roared past. For a split second, the train and car were a blur of metal, smoke, and sound.

As the Mustang cleared the tracks, John caught a glimpse of the freight train in his rearview mirror and smirked—a look of reckless satisfaction, the kind only teenagers on borrowed time can wear.

Gravel crunched under his tires as he turned into a narrow driveway. A modest country house sat ahead, humble and familiar.

Before the engine even died, the front door slammed open.

Cynthia Murphy burst out, her ponytail swinging behind her like a whip. She was eighteen and in a hurry, clutching a large pink suitcase in one hand as she raced toward the car.

John didn't even have time to ask before she was in the passenger seat.

"Hey babe!" he said, leaning in for a kiss.

Cynthia shot him a glare that froze him in place. "Go," she said sharply. "Just go. My dad's in one of his moods again."

John blinked. "What the hell?"

No further explanation needed. He slammed the Mustang into reverse, tires spitting gravel as they tore back out onto the road.

They didn't speak for a mile. The road wound through the rolling countryside, trees painted in golden October hues, but neither of them looked out the window.

John finally broke the silence. "Babe, what's wrong?"

Cynthia didn't look at him. "He said he doesn't want me seeing you anymore. Said you're a pothead with no future."

John let out a breath and turned up the radio.

Then—*hehehe*.

A quiet, unmistakable giggle came from the back seat.

John's eyes darted to the rearview mirror. Cynthia turned her head slowly.

"What the...?" John muttered.

He reached back with one hand and yanked a yellow camping tent off the backseat, revealing a pale, wiry figure crouched behind it.

"Jimmy!?" John barked.

Seventeen-year-old Jimmy Summers—John's little brother—sat frozen, eyes wide behind his Kentucky Wildcats hoodie.

"I... I just wanted to go camping too," Jimmy mumbled.

Cynthia recoiled, her lip curling. "Eww. Were you gonna hide in the woods and film us for your YouTube channel?"

"No! I just— I thought it'd be cool to hang out..." John slammed the brakes and pulled off to the side of the road. He twisted in his seat, straining to reach his brother.

"You little dweeb! I oughta... Get OUT! Now!"

"But how am I supposed to get home?" Jimmy protested.

"Hell if I know! Text one of your dorky friends!"

Cynthia didn't say anything, though a flicker of sympathy crossed her face.

Jimmy grabbed his backpack and climbed out of the car, slamming the door with all the force he could muster.

"You're a jerk," he muttered.

"Get out, loser," John growled.

They watched him for a beat—alone, small, and furious on the roadside.

"You didn't have to be so mean," Cynthia said softly. "He looks up to you."

John turned away in a huff. "That little turd's gonna get it when I get back home."

He twisted the volume knob hard. Metallica's growl filled the car again as the Mustang peeled out, gravel scattering behind them.

Back on the road, Jimmy stood still.

"POTHEAD!" he shouted at the fading yellow blur.

Then he sighed and started the long walk home.

I Got a Knife...

The woods stretched out like a cathedral of bare limbs, their branches clawing at the overcast sky. Leaves crackled beneath each step as John Summers led the way, burdened with a lopsided load of gear. A yellow camping tent was slung over one shoulder, a faded backpack pulled awkwardly across his back, and Cynthia's oversized pink suitcase—almost comically large—swung from his left hand.

Ahead, the silhouette of a towering train trestle loomed through the trees like a rusted monument. The forest was quiet, save for the scuff of boots and the faint metal clink of zippers brushing against each other.

Cynthia glanced over, her brow creasing. "I can carry one of those bags."

John gave her a half-grin and shifted the weight. "Nah, I got it." The words came out through a forced smile as he adjusted the load with a grunt.

"Why'd you pack so much?" he teased. "We're just gonna be gone one night."

"I don't know," Cynthia said, shrugging. "I've never been camping before. Didn't know what to bring." John nodded toward the trestle. "We should climb up, check out the view."

"I'm not too big on heights," she replied, her eyes avoiding the metal skeleton in the distance.

They trudged deeper until they reached a small clearing where sunlight trickled through the canopy. Fallen leaves carpeted the ground in shades of orange and brown, untouched and still.

John stopped. "How about we set up camp here? Looks like a good spot."

Cynthia glanced around, then nodded. "Sure..."

Suddenly — *snap*.

A sharp crack cut through the stillness. Cynthia whipped around. John flinched and dropped the suitcase with a thud before catching himself, trying to play it cool.

"What was that?" she asked, her voice tight.

"Probably just a squirrel," he muttered.

A moment later, a strange *bleat* echoed through the trees behind them — sharp, nasal, unnatural.

They turned again.

John scanned the edge of the clearing and pulled a pocket knife from his jeans, flicking it open with a practiced motion. "Don't worry," he said, a little too loud. "Ain't nothing gonna bother us out here."

Cynthia moved closer, slipping her hand into his.

He gave her a reassuring nod. "C'mon. Let's build a fire before it gets dark."

She hesitated, then nodded.

◆ ◆ ◆ ◆ ◆ ◆

By dusk, the forest had turned to shadow. Thin streaks of orange sunlight filtered through the trees, catching on the beams of the distant trestle. The fire John built crackled low in a pit of gathered stones. Cicadas buzzed in chorus. A soft breeze stirred the dry leaves just beyond the clearing.

John slouched on a fallen log in front of the yellow tent, holding a marshmallow lazily over the fire, watching it blister and char. He wasn't paying much attention. His eyes kept drifting toward Cynthia.

She sat beside him, close but distracted, scrolling through her phone. The flickering firelight danced on her face.

"You're so hot," John said, smirking.

Cynthia looked up, her lips curling into a mischievous grin. She pocketed her phone and leaned in to kiss him.

But something rustled behind them.

Not leaves in the wind. Not an animal darting. Footsteps.

Cynthia froze, her eyes darting toward the trees. "Did you hear that?"

John chuckled, playing it off. "Probably some kind of critter." He shifted his tone, grinning. "Might be Bigfoot."

She wasn't laughing.

John draped his arm around her. "There's nothing out here but us and a bunch of trees."

She pointed toward the trestle, now nearly swallowed by dusk. "I saw a video on YouTube. They say there's some kind of creature that lives up there."

John rolled his eyes.

Rustle.

This one was closer.

Cynthia sat upright. "Shhh. No… listen. That sound again."

They both went still.

In the distance: a low, sickly *bleat*. Twisted and wrong.

John squinted into the darkness. "That sounded like a goat."

Cynthia's voice trembled. "No. That's not right. My family had goats growing up. That... that sounded sick. Like it wasn't coming from an animal."

He stood, squinting, tension gathering in his jaw. "It's probably my little brother trying to scare us."

But his voice lacked conviction.

"I don't like this," Cynthia whispered. "Maybe we should just pack up and go home."

He kissed her quickly and stepped away. "Hey, I'll check it out. Be right back."

"Don't go far," she said, barely audible.

"Be right back, babe."

Then he disappeared into the trees, swallowed by shadow.

John pushed deeper into the woods, phone flashlight cutting a pale cone through the underbrush. His pocketknife gleamed faintly in his other hand, though his grip trembled more than he cared to admit. The woods pressed in around him, every branch scratching across his jacket like skeletal fingers.

"Alright, knock it off!" he called, his voice hard but thin in the stillness.

"Jimmy? That you?"

The only answer was the groan of branches swaying overhead.

Ahead, a cluster of large rocks jutted from the earth, half-hidden by brush. Something about the shadows between them caught his eye. He stepped closer, straining to see. Then…

Bleat.

Closer this time. Strange and warbling, carrying a distorted echo through the trees. John froze, sucking in a shallow breath.

"I got a knife," he warned the dark. "I don't want no trouble, alright?"

Suddenly, a harsh *snort* tore through the silence.

Leaves shifted, rustling fast. John spun, bracing…

A small goat darted out from beneath the brush, bleating as it bounded into the open. John's breath whooshed out in a half-laugh, half-swear.

"You scared me, little fella."

The goat glanced back, then scampered into the trees. Grinning, John turned toward the glow of the campfire-

And froze.

From the shadows, something lunged. Low. Fast.

Too big, too wrong to be an animal.

"WHAT THE…!?"

The impact slammed into him, knocking the knife and phone spinning into the leaves. He hit the ground hard, air ripped from his lungs. A hairy, iron grip clamped onto his shoulder. Then teeth sank into his throat.

John's scream was strangled, choked into silence. Warmth poured across his chest, soaking the leaves beneath him. He gurgled once, twice, then lay still as the dark shape hunched over him, feeding.

Back at the fire, Cynthia sat stiffly on the log, phone in hand, the blue light painting her trembling face. She glanced up toward the woods, straining to hear.

"John?"

No reply. Just the hiss of cicadas and the soft crackle of burning wood.

Her voice rose. "JOHN!?"

Still nothing.

She stood, heart hammering, her eyes darting across the tree line. The shadows shifted with every gust of wind. She swallowed hard, hugging herself.

Then she heard it — the snap of branches. Heavy. Fast. Something charging through the dark.

Her head whipped toward the sound. A silhouette burst into view between the trees, its limbs too long, moving with a hideous gallop. A shape both human and beast.

"John!?" Cynthia's voice cracked, trembling on the edge of panic.

The shadows erupted. Something charged through the trees with a thunder of snapping branches, its limbs long and crooked, its silhouette moving like no animal she knew. It covered the clearing in seconds.

Cynthia's scream was muffled as the thing hit her, a blur of bristled hair and raw power. She thrashed once, twice — then a wet gurgle broke from her throat as the creature's weight pressed her down. The air filled with the sick, metallic scent of blood.

A sound tore from the monster's chest, high-pitched and piercing — an unholy bleat, sharp enough to rattle the branches overhead. Then, just as suddenly, it was gone, slipping back into the dark with a speed that seemed impossible, dragging the night in its wake.

The fire crackled. The woods went still.

At the edge of the firelight, Cynthia's white tennis shoe twitched once in the dirt. Then it sagged lifelessly. Blood sprayed across the yellow nylon of the tent, dripping in thick, uneven streaks, as if a wild hand had painted the canvas with crimson.

Bodies

The electronics store buzzed under harsh fluorescent lights, too bright for Shelley White's taste. Rows of humming TVs and glowing phone displays made the place feel sterile, like a hospital that only sold screens.

She trailed past a counter of the latest smartphones, black nails drumming absently on the glass. Her black hoodie was patched with band logos, her skirt layered over ripped tights, a deliberate clash of style that made her look untouchable to most people. But the way she paused to smile faintly at a mother wrestling with her toddler near the service desk betrayed the truth — Shelley wasn't half as intimidating as she looked.

"Excuse me," she asked a clerk in a blue polo, "what's the newest phone you've got? Like, the top one?"

The clerk brightened, leading her toward a glass counter filled with sleek models. "We just got the newest Galaxy in," he said, tapping the display. "Camera's insane. Practically professional quality."

Shelley leaned closer, eyeing the glowing screen, but a sudden shift of sound pulled her attention away. Across the store, in the TV section, all the displays cut to the same logo: **WLKL-13 Kentucky Eyewitness News.** The anchor's calm voice rose above the chatter of customers.

"We have some breaking news this afternoon. The bodies of two young adults were discovered earlier this morning in the Pope Lick Creek area, just south of the old train trestle..."

Shelley drifted toward the wall of televisions. On thirty screens at once, shaky footage of police tape and flashing blue lights filled the air. A coroner's van idled behind the trees.

The picture shifted to a roadside press conference. Chief Hodges stood there, a man weathered by decades in uniform, his jaw set like stone. Next to him, Trey Robertson held a microphone, polished and eager, his newsman smile flickering.

"This is an active crime scene," Hodges barked. "We're still trying to figure out what happened here last night. I don't have nothing else to say."

"Chief, can you tell us—" Trey pressed.

"Damn it, son, we *are* going to get to the bottom of this." Hodges' voice thundered across the screens before he turned and stormed off. Trey froze, lips parting, thrown off his rhythm.

The broadcast cut back to the anchor, who shuffled his papers with the hint of a smirk.

"But this isn't the first time strange deaths have occurred near Pope Lick..."

Then came the testimony of an old man outside a sun-bleached gas station, his eyes sharp with conviction. "That thing's been out there since I was a boy. It's half-man, half-beast! Some kind of army experiment with radiation that went wrong in the woods."

The studio lights returned, the anchor chuckling softly.

"Wild theories, indeed."

But then his tone darkened, sober, steady.

"For the families of the victims, this is no urban legend. We'll keep you updated with official information from the police investigation as details develop."

The segment ended with the familiar newsroom jingle.

Shelley stood frozen in front of the wall of TVs, her reflection multiplied thirty times over in the glow of the screens. Pope Lick. She'd heard whispers of the stories her whole life — the trestle, the thing in the woods, the people who never came back.

But this was different. This was real.

◆ ◆ ◆ ◆ ◆ ◆

The sky pressed low and gray, the clouds hanging heavy over Pope Lick Park. A line of uniformed officers moved slowly through the trees in formation, fluorescent tape markers dangling from their belts, radios crackling softly.

Chief Hodges kept his hand hooked on his belt as he scanned the undergrowth. His eyes were sharp, practiced, he'd walked scenes like this too many times before. But the woods at Pope Lick felt different. Kind of like something was watching.

A few yards off the line, Officer Cole crouched beneath a low limb. He paused by a moss-covered log, something catching his eye.

"Got something," Cole called out.

He reached beneath the damp wood and drew out a mud-caked cell phone. Its screen was spiderwebbed with cracks, black mud packed along the edges.

"It's a phone," he muttered, brushing off the muck.

Behind him, in the shadows between the trees, something stirred. A tall shape rose slowly, silently. Its outline was vaguely human — but twisted and hunched. Motionless. Watching.

The phone buzzed suddenly in Cole's hand. *BZZZZ. BZZZZ.*

He jolted, nearly dropping it, his heart spiking against his ribs. The cracked screen flickered to life. The words glowed in fractured glass: **INCOMING CALL – SCAM LIKELY.**

Cole exhaled a shaky breath. "Jesus..."

"What've you got?" Hodges' voice cut through the trees as he approached.

Cole turned, still gripping the buzzing phone. "One of the kids' phones, sir."

Hodges stepped closer. "Bag it. We'll check for prints or messages—"

He stopped. His head turned sharply toward the trees.

Movement. Just there.

The officers fell quiet, listening. The branches whispered as if stirred by something more than wind. Cole glanced back over his shoulder. The dark figure that had stood behind him was gone.

"You see someone back here?" Hodges asked, his voice low, dangerous.

Cole shook his head. "No, sir."

But the tightness in his voice betrayed the truth— he *had* felt it too.

Hodges kept his gaze sweeping the brush, every line of his face carved deeper with unease. Finally, he growled: "Keep moving. Eyes sharp. I want this whole area cleared before sunset."

He took a step and paused, spotting the trestle. "This damn place again..."

Cole glanced up at the iron silhouette. "Heard the same stories all my life, sir. The Goatman."

Hodges gave a humorless snort. "People see what they want to see. There have been sightings of wild goats out here for years, escaped from a farm up the creek." He shook his head. "I've been doing this a long time, Cole. Been out here more times than I can count. There is no Goatman. When we found a body, it was always some teenager who got drunk, went looking for a monster after seeing a stray goat, and either got hit by a train or fell off the damn thing." His jaw tightened. "An urban legend is the last thing we need right now."

The line of officers pushed on, their boots squelching in unison, their radios crackling faintly as the woods closed in tighter around them.

And in the shadows they left behind, something unseen lingered. Watching. Waiting.

♦ ♦ ♦ ♦ ♦ ♦

The car was silent but for the low hum of the tires on asphalt. The trip to the funeral home wasn't long, but to Jimmy it felt endless, stretched out by the weight pressing against his chest. He sat in the back seat, forehead against the cool glass of the window, watching the blur of trees and powerlines roll past without really seeing them. His eyes stung, raw and tired.

Up front, his father, Barry, kept both hands tight on the wheel. Beside him, Jimmy's mother, Sandra, twisted a tissue in her lap, dabbing at her swollen eyes. "You're going too slow."

"We won't be late," Barry replied evenly, eyes on the road.

"You're barely doing the speed limit. For God's sake, can't you go a little faster?"

Barry tightened his grip on the wheel. "There's a police car right behind us. You want me to give him a reason to pull us over on the way to our own son's visitation?"

Sandra sighed, frustrated, pressing the tissue hard to her eyes. "I just want to make sure we get there on time."

She fell quiet for a beat, then added, almost frantically, "And the house—there's barely any food. You know people are going to come over, and we've got nothing to eat."

Barry rolled his eyes, but he kept his voice steady. "We'll figure it out."

His calmness only seemed to needle her more. Sandra let out a shaky breath, crumpling the tissue in her fist.

From the back seat, Jimmy finally spoke, his voice soft and raw. "Let's just… get through the next few hours."

Silence filled the car again. Barry looked at him through the rearview mirror and gave a small nod. "He's right."

Sandra turned her face toward the window, shoulders trembling. Jimmy leaned his head back against the seat and shut his eyes. The car rolled on, carrying all three of them toward the place they least wanted to go.

The funeral home smelled faintly of lilies and polished wood. Muted lamps cast their soft light across the visitation room, giving everything a glow that was warm but unbearably heavy. From overhead, a hymn drifted through tinny speakers, the kind of song no one really heard but everyone felt.

At the front of the room rested a closed mahogany coffin, flanked by wreaths. Beside it stood a framed photograph of John Summers in his senior portrait — clean-shaven, polo shirt tucked into jeans, smiling like the future had already opened its door.

Jimmy stood near the coffin with his parents. His eyes were glassy and red, locked on the carpet as though staring at it might keep him from breaking apart.

Sandra clutched a crumpled tissue in both hands, her sobs leaking out despite every effort to hold them in. Barry stood rigid as stone, his jaw clenched like if he opened his mouth even once he might never stop yelling at the universe.

Jimmy trembled beside him, barely perceptible, until his father shifted slightly and wrapped an arm around his son's shoulders. It was a rare gesture — stiff, awkward, but grounding.

"He loved you, you know," Barry muttered, not looking at him.

Jimmy nodded but didn't speak.

His uncle Arnold stepped up next, the former military man's back still straight as a board even in grief. He squeezed Jimmy's shoulder, offering no words, just a brief wink before moving to the coffin. For a long moment, Arnold stood at the senior portrait, his face tight, before he wiped a tear from his cheek.

Mourners passed in hushed clusters, offering handshakes, brief hugs, fragments of comfort.

Mr. Stringer, one of John's teachers, stepped forward. Short and stout in a worn tweed jacket, his round glasses slipped a little as he patted Jimmy's arm before turning to the parents.

"I want y'all to know... I'm so sorry," he said, voice breaking. "I had John in U.S. History last year. He was..." Stringer stopped, swallowing hard. "He was sharp. And always cracking jokes. Made me, made all the students laugh."

Sandra pressed her hands to her face, overcome. Mr. Stringer shifted back awkwardly, grief tumbling over his words as he retreated.

The room fell into a strained silence, the kind that always seemed to linger between waves of condolences.

At the back of the room, a figure lingered.

Shelley White.

Today she had traded her usual torn band tees for a black skirt and dark blazer, but the combat boots still clicked softly against the tile as she stepped forward. She didn't join the line of mourners. Instead, her gaze cut straight to Jimmy.

She waited until the space around him thinned, then approached with quiet purpose.

"Hey," she said, low and urgent.

Jimmy blinked, startled, looking up at the girl he thought he had seen at school.

"I'm sorry about John," she added, her voice softened now.

He nodded, uncertain who she was.

"I need to talk to you." A pause. Her eyes locked on his. "Meet me at the Starbucks. Tomorrow night. Eight-thirty. Be there."

She didn't wait for his answer. Just turned and slipped through the side door, her boots echoing as they faded into silence.

Jimmy stared after her, wondering for a moment if he had imagined it.

His father's hand tightened on his shoulder. "You okay?" Barry asked.

Jimmy didn't reply. He just kept staring at the door, curious as to what the cute goth girl wanted to talk to him about.

◆ ◆ ◆ ◆ ◆ ◆

By the time the last cluster of mourners trickled out of the Summers' house, the place felt like a balloon slowly losing air. Coats rustled, doors clicked shut, murmured condolences faded down the driveway. The living room, once buzzing with bodies and casseroles, now sagged in the quiet.

Jimmy sat on the couch, his uncle Arnold beside him, both scrolling absently through their phones as if staring at screens could shield them from the weight of the day.

Across the room, Barry leaned against the mantel, a glass of whiskey in his hand. He wasn't drunk—not yet—but the way he turned the glass between his fingers showed he had already had a few drinks.

Arnold slid his phone back into his pocket, then gave Jimmy's shoulder a pat before standing. "Gotta go, bud."

Jimmy looked up, managing a faint nod.

Arnold turned to his brother. "I'm heading home." He reached for the door, then paused, glancing back with a half-grin. "Saturday… we're still on for the game, right?"

For the first time in what felt like forever, Barry's lips twitched into something resembling a smile. He let out a small snicker, the sound foreign but welcome. "Kentucky's only a three-point favorite," he said.

Arnold scoffed. "C'mon. It's Vanderbilt." He chuckled to himself, then gave a final wave. "See you Saturday."

The door shut behind him, leaving father and son in the stillness.

Jimmy rose from the couch. Barry looked at him, glass in hand. "You okay?"

Jimmy hesitated, then tried to smile. "Yeah. Just… a little sad."

Barry nodded, his eyes softer than before. "I know. Me too."

Jimmy slipped away down the hall.

His bedroom felt smaller than usual, the air heavy with the residue of the wake. Jimmy sat at his desk, phone in hand, staring at the glowing screen. His YouTube channel page filled the display: *J. SUMMERTIME.*

The thumbnails glared back at him in loud colors and exaggerated faces. *EPIC FIREWORKS FAIL. I ATE A GHOST PEPPER AND INSTANTLY REGRETTED IT. HOW LONG CAN I LICK A 9 VOLT BATTERY.*

Subscriber count: 202.

A cheap poster with his channel name drooped against the wall behind him, corners curling where the tape had peeled away.

Jimmy sighed. All of it felt like someone else's life—bright, silly, shallow. A world that didn't exist anymore.

He adjusted the phone into its tripod. His expression hardened, a seriousness rarely seen in front of his camera. Taking a steadying breath, he pressed record.

"So," he began, voice low, "I don't know if you've heard, but my big brother was killed the other day. Out in the woods." His eyes flicked away for a moment, then back to the lens. "Police don't know much. Some say it was… some kind of monster."

He leaned back, exhaling. "Me and my brother didn't get along. But I loved him." His throat tightened. "I'm gonna miss him."

The silence stretched. Jimmy reached forward and tapped stop. The phone chirped as the recording saved. He sank into his chair, head in his hands.

But something unsettled him. A thought, a spark, something that wouldn't leave. He sat back up, took a deep breath. He hit record again.

His voice was firmer now. "I'm not sure if it's a monster out there. But I'm gonna find out what it is." He paused, leaning closer to the lens. "For John."

The red recording light glowed on his face, catching the seriousness in his eyes.

◆ ◆ ◆ ◆ ◆ ◆

Down the hall, Sandra took the framed picture of John that had been used at the wake and walked toward his bedroom. Like she had done a thousand times before, she opened the door and turned on the light. She walked around the room, her eyes scanning the familiar chaos. A Kentucky Wildcats basketball pennant was tacked to the wall, next to a small trophy from his time on the high school baseball team. On the dresser sat a paper plate with a few stale potato chips left on it, and two dirty socks lay tossed in the middle of the floor. She took it all in — the casual, lived-in mess of a life still in progress. And then it hit her. A quiet cry turned into a gut-wrenching sob.

Barry rushed in to find her sitting on the edge of the bed, clutching John's football letterman jacket. He stood in the doorway, his own grief a stone in his throat, unsure what to say.

"He's never coming home," she said through her tears. "He's really gone…"

Barry sat down beside his wife, his body heavy, fighting back the tears that burned his own eyes. Sandra raised the jacket to her nose, inhaling deeply. "It still smells like him…," she cried, burying her face in the fabric.

Hearing the commotion, Jimmy appeared in the doorway. He saw his mother crying, his dad fighting to hold himself together, and his own throat tightened. Sandra looked up, saw the pain on her youngest son's face, and tried to compose herself, wiping at her eyes. "Oh, honey," she said, her voice thick. "I didn't mean to upset you."

Jimmy crossed the room and sat on the bed. He and his father wrapped their arms around her, the three of them holding on to each other in the center of the room, sharing the crushing weight of their sorrow.

Banana Nut

The smell of coffee and pumpkin spice clung to the air as Jimmy stepped into Starbucks. Each time the glass doors opened, a cool October breeze rolled in, carrying the rustle of fallen leaves. The shop was busy but not crowded—students hunched over laptops, friends chatting in pairs, a few customers in University of Louisville red or Kentucky blue, their team gear standing out like flags in enemy territory.

Jimmy pulled at the sleeves of his own Kentucky hoodie as he scanned the room. His jeans were faded, sneakers scuffed, his posture sagging under grief that clung like an extra weight. Spotting an open table near the front windows, he slipped into the chair, restless.

His eyes wandered—watching a barista scribble names on cups, lingering on the glowing pastry case though he wasn't hungry. He pulled out his phone to kill some time, then blinked at the screen. His subscriber count had ticked up. *202… 239.* A strange little jolt of life moved through him.

"Hey."

The voice came from behind, soft but sudden. Jimmy turned, startled.

Shelley stood there, almost ghostlike in the warm glow of the café lights. Black skirt, dark blazer, heavy eyeliner—her rocker edge toned down but never absent. She slid into the seat across from him, setting down a small brown Starbucks bag and a laptop.

"You get a muffin or something?" Jimmy asked.

"Banana nut," she said with a short nod.

"Cool."

The silence stretched, awkward and heavy. She tore off a piece of the muffin and took a bite, then set it down deliberately.

"I meant what I said yesterday," Shelley said, her voice lowering, softer than her appearance suggested. "About being sorry. Your brother… he was kind of a goofball. But he made people laugh." She smiled faintly at the memory. "I had home ec with him sophomore year. He once flung pancake batter onto the ceiling. It stayed up there 'til spring break."

Jimmy almost smiled. "Yeah. That sounds like him."

Her face grew more serious. "Anyway, I didn't just want to say sorry. I asked you here because of something else."

She leaned forward, her voice dropping. "I saw the news. They threw in that bit about an urban legend — some army science experiment gone bad or whatever."

"Yeah," Jimmy said. "I've heard stuff like that all my life."

Shelley's eyes narrowed slightly, skeptical but intent. "When I was in middle school, one of my classmates' dads went missing. He went hunting in the woods one morning. Never came back. They found one of his boots out by the creek."

Jimmy leaned in, his heart thudding a little faster.

"My grandpa used to tell me a story," Shelley continued. "When I was little. About a train wreck. A circus train, back in the seventies. He said he was in it when it derailed near Pope Lick Creek. Some animals escaped. A few people didn't make it." She paused, letting the weight settle. "What if there's something really out there? Something that's been out there since the wreck?"

Jimmy stared, unsure if she was serious, but unable to look away.

"Like some wild animal," Shelley said slowly.

His face shifted — uncertainty, fear, and something else: curiosity. "You really think… something got him?"

"I don't know," Shelley admitted. "But I do know my grandpa's still alive. He lives across the river, in New Albany. Retirement home called Willow Glen. He remembers stuff." She leaned closer. "If you want to talk to him… I'll take you."

Jimmy looked out the window, cars sliding past in the night, their headlights smearing across the glass. He tapped his fingers against the table.

"Okay," he said finally. "Yeah. I think I do. You think I could… interview him? For my channel?"

She tilted her head. "I dunno. We can ask him."

Jimmy nodded, already feeling the pull of something bigger than him taking shape.

"Tomorrow," Shelley said, pushing back her chair. "Meet me at the library at four. I want to look into something before we go see him."

She tossed her empty bag into the trash, her combat boots clicking softly across the tile. At the door she turned, meeting his eyes one last time.

"I'll drive."

Then she was gone, leaving Jimmy staring at the reflection of himself in the darkened window, the muffled hum of the café fading into the background.

◆ ◆ ◆ ◆ ◆ ◆

Muted autumn light spilled through the curtains, soft and tired. On the mounted TV, Kentucky football stumbled their way through another Saturday, the scoreline ugly and familiar: **Vanderbilt 17 – Kentucky 13.**

Jimmy slouched on the couch in a Kentucky cap, legs tucked under him, half-watching the game, half-scrolling on his phone. His heart wasn't in it, but the game filled the silence, and that was something.

Barry leaned against the recliner, a sweating Bud Light clutched loosely in his hand. Beside Jimmy, Uncle Arnold hunched forward with laser focus, a Sam Adams bottle dangling between his fingers.

"...and it's another first down for Vanderbilt," the announcer groaned through the speakers. "And with that the Commodores can take a knee and run out the clock. The Cats have now lost three straight with Alabama coming to Lexington in two weeks.

Arnold slapped his knee and barked at the screen. "Dammit! How did they leave that kid, Eighty-two, wide open all day?"

Barry smirked faintly. "Their secondary's struggling."

"I can't believe we lost to Vanderbilt," Arnold muttered, shaking his head. He glared at the score like it was a personal insult. "Again..."

He stood abruptly, tossing his hands in the air. "Unbelievable." Muttering curses under his breath, he stormed toward the kitchen, fishing his phone out of his pocket.

Barry and Jimmy exchanged a look. Barry shrugged. "He's been that way all his life. Thank God for basketball season."

Jimmy almost smiled. Then he pushed himself off the couch.

Sandra appeared in the hallway, folding dish towels as Jimmy passed. She caught him heading for the front door.

"Where you goin'?" she asked.

Jimmy paused, hand on the knob. "Just... going to see a friend."

Her eyebrow lifted. "Is it a girl?"

Jimmy stiffened, his voice too quick. "No. Just—just a friend of John's. We met at the visitation."

Sandra studied him. Her eyes were swollen from crying, but a trace of warmth flickered through the sorrow. She gave a small, tired smile. "Well... don't be out too late."

Jimmy nodded. "I won't."

The screen door creaked shut behind him. Sandra lingered for a moment, staring at the empty doorway, then turned back toward the kitchen.

The kitchen smelled faintly of coffee and fried food from earlier in the day. A half-empty can of Pringles sat abandoned on the counter. The steady tick of the wall clock filled the silence.

Barry stepped in, beer still in hand, phone in the other. Arnold sat at the table, two empty Bud Lights in front of him, his eyes glued to a video on his phone.

"Losing to Vanderbilt sucks," Barry said with a sigh, "but if we beat Tennessee in a few weeks, I'll call it a decent season."

Arnold didn't look up.

Barry chuckled, shaking his head.

Arnold finally spoke, his eyes still on the screen. "You ever seen this guy? He's got this whole channel about Kentucky monsters. Listen to this..."

He tapped the screen. A tinny voice filled the kitchen, paired with grainy footage of foggy woods and shaky shots of the Pope Lick trestle.

"*...and some say the Goatman was no myth. A half-man, half-goat hybrid — created in a lab right here in Kentucky. The story goes, the scientist couldn't control it... so he took the creature out into the woods. It was his creation. He couldn't kill it... so he left it there.*"

Barry barked out a laugh. "Come on. This dude's got, what, fifteen followers? Thinks Bigfoot and Mothman are cousins."

He glanced up — only to see Arnold's expression. Not amused. Focused.

The video continued.

"*...but with the recent murders in Pope Lick park, some locals believe the legend is real. That something's still out there. It is out there lurking. Watching. When will it strike again?*"

Barry raised an eyebrow. "Oh no. Don't tell me you're buyin' this."

Arnold stood slowly, the phone screen dimming in his hand. His jaw worked as if chewing on something he didn't want to say. "Just reminded me I got a few things to work on around the house."

Barry eyed him. "What kind of things?"

Arnold didn't answer. He grabbed another Bud Light from the fridge, shutting the door with more force than necessary. His eyes caught briefly on a magnet holding up a faded photo of Jimmy and John as children, smiling with silly gap-toothed grins. Arnold's face tightened. He exhaled sharply, then turned and walked off.

Barry watched him leave, the grin gone from his face. He muttered into the empty kitchen: "...you better not be thinkin' of goin' out there."

World of Wonders

The Louisville Free Public Library breathed with quiet. Sunlight streamed through tall windows, catching dust motes that drifted like tiny stars in the still air. Wooden tables stretched between the stacks, filled with students hunched over laptops and retirees leafing through newspapers. The place had the calm weight of a cathedral — only the gods here were ink and paper.

Jimmy and Shelley walked up to the main reference desk, where a librarian with sharp, intelligent eyes looked up over a pair of reading glasses.

"Excuse me," Shelley began. "We need to look at some old local newspapers."

The librarian gave them a polite smile. "Of course. Which years are you looking for?"

"1978," Jimmy answered.

Shelley leaned in slightly. "We're trying to find information on a train crash."

The librarian's smile faltered. "Oh, for a paper?"

"We think it's linked to the Goatman," Shelley added in a hushed voice.

The librarian's eyebrow shot up over the rim of her glasses. She leaned forward, lowering her own voice conspiratorially. "The train crash is one version. I always heard that there was a farmer in the area who did experiments on goats. They say one night, after years of experiments on one of them, it killed the farmer and escaped and has been living down by the creek somewhere." She straightened up, her professional demeanor returning. "But that's just a story, of course. The microfilm archives are in the back."

A few minutes later, Jimmy and Shelley sat shoulder-to-shoulder at a microfilm reader, the machine humming softly as reels spun and stopped under Jimmy's careful crank. A small stack of canisters sat between them, their labels faded from decades of use. Shelley's phone glowed faintly in her hand, the screen filled with dates she had scrawled into a note.

"Okay," she whispered, her eyeliner-dark eyes fixed on the glass, "the official report on the Pope Lick derailment is October '78. But there's almost nothing about a circus."

Jimmy kept scrolling, his face tense with concentration. "Your grandfather wouldn't make it up, would he?"

"No," Shelley said without hesitation. "Maybe it was a smaller, independent show. Not Ringling Brothers. Try searching for 'sideshow.' Or 'freak show.'"

Jimmy nodded, his fingers fumbling slightly as he swapped out the roll. The screen flickered with black-and-white frames—advertisements, obituaries, the usual parade of local politics. He cranked slowly, and then—"Whoa," he breathed. "Got something."

Shelley leaned closer, her shoulder brushing his as they bent toward the screen. Together they stared at the small, blocky print of a newspaper ad:

STETSON STERLING'S WORLD OF WONDERS – MARVELS TO ASTONISH!
Louisville, October 29th through 31st.

Shelley's lips parted. "That has to be it." She tapped her phone. "See? Now check the days before the show."

Jimmy scrolled back. The microfilm whirred, lines of text blurring past until he stopped at a short article, almost lost in the clutter of the back pages.

The headline read: **ONE DEAD, ONE MISSING AFTER TRAIN DERAILS.**

Jimmy's breath caught. He leaned closer, reading the tiny words. "Just a paragraph. But it says the World of Wonders was traveling from Cincinnati."

They turned to each other at the same time, the glow of the screen reflected in their eyes. The discovery hung between them, heavy, undeniable.

Jimmy broke the silence first. "Let's go talk to your grandpa."

Shelley nodded, her expression firm, resolved. For the first time, she looked less like the aloof goth girl and more like someone carrying a purpose.

◆ ◆ ◆ ◆ ◆ ◆

The lobby of Willow Glen smelled faintly of antiseptic and lemon polish. The muted lighting gave everything a hazy softness, but it didn't hide the tired vinyl chairs, the fake greenery in every corner, or the disinterested receptionist bent intently over her crossword puzzle.

The elevator dinged and the doors slid open. Jimmy and Shelley stepped out, their sneakers squeaking across the polished linoleum.

"Room two-twelve," Shelley murmured. "Down this way."

They moved past closed doors, muted televisions whispering behind some of them. A chess game sat abandoned on a nearby table, pieces mid-battle, as if the players had simply never returned.

Abe's room was neat, the sort of order that comes with long routine. A window overlooked a quiet courtyard where the last of the autumn leaves swirled in circles. Family photos in mismatched frames lined the dresser. A cane rested against a floral armchair like an extension of the man who owned it.

Abe was there, hunched over a crossword book on his lap. Even seated, he seemed too large for the room, his long legs stretching out awkwardly in front of him. When the door opened, his head lifted, and his lined face lit up.

"Shelley?"

He rose slowly, awkwardly, leaning hard on the cane—but when he stood, his height was still striking, almost unnatural.

"Well, I'll be!" he said warmly. "C'mere."

Shelley darted forward and hugged him. Abe leaned down, his massive arm folding around her with surprising gentleness.

"I believe you get prettier every time I see you," he said.

"I've missed you," Shelley whispered.

"I've missed you too, sweetheart."

Jimmy hovered just inside the doorway, unsure of where to stand, his eyes widening as he tried to process just how tall Shelley's grandfather really was.

"This is Jimmy," Shelley said, stepping back.

"He's... well, he's a friend of mine."

Abe gave him a nod. "Hello there."

"Hello, sir," Jimmy managed.

"Please," Abe said, flashing a smile that made his face look years younger. "Call me Abe."

Jimmy nodded quickly.

"Sit," Abe said, motioning toward the chairs. "Both of you."

They settled across from him. A bowl of M&Ms sat on the table between them, bright against the muted colors of the room.

"You want some?" Abe asked.

Jimmy shook his head politely. Shelley plucked a yellow one and tossed it in her mouth. Abe followed suit, plucking a green candy and crunching it between his teeth.

There was a pause, the hum of silence only broken by the faint ticking of a wall clock. Shelley leaned forward.

"Grandpa... remember that story you used to tell me? When I was little? Wasn't there a bad train crash in Louisville?"

The change in Abe's face was instant. His smile fell, his eyes drifting toward the courtyard window as if the memory itself stood waiting out there among the bare trees.

"Yeah," he said quietly. "I remember." He tapped his cane once against the floor, voice dropping. "I'll never forget it."

Shelley glanced at Jimmy, then back to her grandfather. "Would you mind telling it for Jimmy's YouTube channel?"

Abe's brow furrowed. He scratched the side of his head. "For... the internet?" He chuckled once, a hollow sound. "I don't know, honey."

"Please," Shelley said gently, her tone half-daughterly, half-coaxing.

Abe rubbed a hand across his thinning hair, exhaled long through his nose. Finally, he leaned back in his chair, his huge frame settling into the cushions. His eyes darkened with the weight of memory.

"It was forty years ago..."

The World's Tallest Man

The cavernous hall of Cincinnati's Union Terminal hummed with the shuffle of travelers, the murmur of voices rising beneath its vaulted ceiling. But near Gate 7, the usual flow of passengers had slowed, curiosity drawing them into a crowd. People craned their necks, whispering, staring at a peculiar group that stood apart from the rest.

Abe's voice carried over the memory, older now, softened with age but still edged with the weight of truth:

"I was part of a traveling sideshow back then. Played the part of the World's Tallest Man. We had just finished our last show in Cincinnati, and that night we were bound for Louisville."

On a worn wooden bench, a much younger Abe sat hunched, knees nearly touching his chin despite his best attempt at folding himself small. His enormous hands struggled with a newspaper, the pages flimsy and inadequate against his frame.

"We were a tight-knit group," he went on. *"Odd to the rest of the world maybe, but to us? We were family."*

Just beyond him, Bobo the Rubber Boy entertained himself by twisting his body in impossible ways, bending arms and legs until he seemed more knot than man.

"Bobo, he was our contortionist. He could move his body like a snake, tie himself into a knot if he wanted. Then there were Sally and Ally — conjoined twins. Sweet girls."

The sisters stood side by side, awkward but polite, smiling stiffly at the gawkers. Ally's eyes flicked toward Abe, and when he offered the faintest smile back, her own grew shy and lingering.

"Dated Ally for a while," Abe admitted. *"But that's another story."*

Nearby, Lil' Margie, a 50-year-old little person preened in a hand mirror, dolled up like an actress from the silver-screen. She wore her Hollywood memories proudly, her handbag stuffed with old headshots.

"Lil' Margie was short of stature," Abe recalled. *"But she was glamourous. Margie appeared in a Humphrey Bogart film as a kid. She milked that starlet bit for thirty or forty years."*

A little girl, clutching a program in both hands, edged forward.

"Can I… can I have your autograph, ma'am?" she asked.

Margie beamed, pulling out an 8x10 of herself, young and glamorous. "Of course, darling. What's your name?"

"Virginia."

Margie scribbled a flourish across the photo: *To Virginia, Dream Big! – Lil' Margie.* The child's eyes shone as if she'd been handed treasure.

Abe's voice softened in the telling. *"The kids loved her. She lived for that."*

The crowd rippled suddenly with murmurs and laughter. Some pointed, others sneered. At the center of their attention stood Priscilla, the Bearded Lady. Her dark beard was combed and shining, regal against her fine dress. At her side was a boy, no more than three, with a unibrow thick as a brushstroke and hair covering his chubby arms.

"There was Priscilla, the bearded lady" Abe said. *"Turned more heads than anyone. And her husband, Willie… he was as good as gold, though he had a bit of a temper."*

Willie, short but broad, squared his shoulders in a crisp suit, his small hand gripping Priscilla's protectively. Locals jeered at the child.

"That little boy," someone whispered too loudly. "He's so hairy."

Priscilla scooped the boy into her arms, rubbing his cheek with tender fingers.

"*Matthew,*" Abe recalled, the warmth clear even now. "*Matty Matty, we called him. Sweetest little fella you ever saw. He was quite hairy. Took after his momma.*"

A commotion stirred as a heckler shoved forward, waving a Cincinnati phone book. He hurled it at Willie. "Hey, strong man! Bet you can't tear that in half!"

The crowd roared with laughter. Willie caught it, eyes blazing. Stetson Sterling stepped forward, the ringleader himself, his scarf bright as a flag and grin wider still.

"*Stetson Sterling was our promoter,*" Abe explained, voice tinged with bitterness. "*Kept the whole show running — but he was always thinking about the money.*"

Stetson clapped a hand on Willie's shoulder, turning to the onlookers. "Now, now, friends! You're asking for a tremendous feat of strength! A man of his caliber doesn't perform for free. Five dollars, and you'll witness the impossible!"

Dollar bills appeared, crumpled but eager. Stetson pocketed them with a magician's flourish.

"Mighty Willie," he boomed, "the floor is yours!"

Willie handed his coat to Priscilla and squared up to the book, grunting, straining, playing the part.

"He can't do it!" the heckler shouted.

Willie paused. A slow smirk crept across his face. With a sudden jerk, the phone book split in his hands — *riiiip!* — pages scattering like a white storm.

The crowd gasped, some clapping, others falling silent, suddenly unsure if they'd been mocking the wrong man.

Priscilla leaned in, kissing Willie's cheek, their son tugging proudly at his father's sleeve.

In the background, a gruff man named Rusty Gant cursed at station porters, shoving wagons loaded with animals — tigers, monkeys, cages rattling — onto the train.

Stetson tipped his hat, already scanning the crowd for the next dollar. "And now, ladies and gentlemen, the midnight train to Louisville awaits!"

Willie stepped up to him, hand out.

Stetson's grin never faltered as he slipped the cash into his own pocket. "You'll get your cut."

Willie's back straightened, but he said nothing, retreating back to Priscilla and Matthew.

The troupe gathered their bags, leaving behind a stunned crowd and tattered phone book.

They all boarded the train, the World of Wonders packed into one of the cars, mismatched seats filled with tired bodies and tired laughter.

Abe sat just behind Priscilla and Willie, his long legs stretched out uncomfortably in the aisle. Little Matthew nestled between his parents, laughing at Abe, who made silly faces. Abe leaned forward, ducking the doll behind the seat and popping it back up again with the child's beloved Raggedy Andy doll. Matthew squealed each time, laughter spilling out of him, sweet and unguarded.

"Sometimes on those rides," Abe's voice carried, *"I'd share my M&Ms with him. That kid loved those things."*

Abe reached into his coat pocket and produced a small bag of candies. He shook one an orange piece. Matthew's eyes lit up as Abe extended his massive hand. The boy snatched it and popped it into his mouth, grinning with chocolate-smeared teeth. Willie and Priscilla chuckled, their exhaustion softening in that brief moment.

The whistle blew, steam hissing. With a lurch, the train heaved itself forward. Cincinnati slipped away, its lights fading into the night.

The car rocked gently as rain began to streak the windows. Wind moaned across the hills outside.

Stetson stood in the aisle, tipping his hat with a flourish. His alligator smile hadn't dimmed.

"Bravo!" he declared. "You gave them a show they won't forget. Now onward! We bring the World of Wonders to Kentucky!"

"We were about halfway to Louisville," Abe's voice recalled, *"when the storm blew in."*

Priscilla leaned her head against Willie's shoulder, Matthew already dozing against her arm. Willie lit a cigarette, puffed smoke toward the ceiling, then glanced at the rattling window.

"Storm's picking up," he muttered.

Priscilla smoothed Matthew's hair, her eyes never leaving him. "He always sleeps better in the rain."

Across the aisle, Bobo stretched himself into a pretzel, feet hooked behind his head. Margie offered him a stick of gum with the casual grace of a queen.

"You ever think we'll be treated like normal folk?" she asked.

Bobo shrugged, twisting free of the pose. "Nah. But it pays the bills."

Abe hunched over a book, his shoulders curved like mountains. Sally and Ally shared a flask, giggling under their breath. Ally tried to catch Abe's eye but failed; he was too buried in the page. Rusty snapped his newspaper taut and scanned the headlines, grumbling under his breath.

Stetson sauntered past, clapping Bobo on the shoulder. "We should go see the horses while we're in town. Louisville's got a fine track."

Bobo nodded. Abe perked up. "Ooh... Can I come? I used to love the ponies back home when I was a kid."

"Of course!" Stetson beamed.

Outside, the train tore across the Kentucky hills. The countryside was a jagged silhouette, black against the storm. Lightning lanced through the sky, revealing barns and twisted trees for a heartbeat at a time before the dark swallowed them again.

The rain came harder, battering the windows like claws. The metal walls groaned, rivets popping faintly under the strain. Each thunderclap hit like artillery fire, shaking the car on its bolts.

"We were almost to Louisville when it happened..." Abe's voice trembled in memory.

The lights flickered, buzzing angrily as though trying to hold on.

Priscilla clutched Matthew closer. "I'm getting scared," she whispered to Willie.

"It's just a storm, honey," he said, though his jaw was tight.

Abe glanced out into the night. A smear of lightning illuminated the hills, so close it felt like the train was running headlong into fire. Bobo shivered, pulling his arms around himself. Margie closed her eyes and hummed some old tune, fragile against the roar. Sally and Ally squeezed each other's hands.

Rusty folded his newspaper slowly, leaning toward the glass. "Trees are leanin' hard..." he muttered.

The storm showed no mercy. Rain hammered the wreckage like a thousand nails, steam rising off iron in ghostly hisses.

Then it came.

BOOM.

A blinding flash, a cannon-shot crack of thunder — and then the oak. Its roots loosened by rain, the old giant groaned, split in two by lightning, and toppled squarely across the rails just as the locomotive barreled into the bend.

The conductor's breath caught in his throat. Through the rain-streaked glass he saw the massive trunk crash down in front of them, immovable as a wall. He yanked the brake.

Too late.

The train screamed forward, a bullet with no target but death and destruction.

Impact. Metal shrieked against wood. Cars buckled, snapped, twisted like toys in a cruel child's hands.

Inside, chaos.

Abe's body slammed into the roof. Bobo's agile frame flung across the aisle like a rag doll, his limbs folding at impossible angles. Sally and Ally shrieked as their shared body was hurled against the wall. Seats tore loose, crushing Margie beneath their weight. Priscilla threw her arms around Matthew — too late.

Darkness swallowed everything.

◆ ◆ ◆ ◆ ◆ ◆

When Abe woke, the world was broken. Steam hissed from the mangled engine, smoke curling upward like the last breath of a dying animal. Rain poured in sheets, plastering his clothes to his giant frame.

Priscilla clawed her way out of the wreck, barefoot and bleeding, her hair matted to her face. She staggered into the creek, the water surging waist-high around her, pulling at her skirts. "Matthew! Willie!" she screamed into the storm.

Willie surfaced downstream, coughing, his small body thrashing just to keep his head above water. "Priscilla! I'm here! I'm alright!"

But her eyes were already wild, searching, scouring every shadow of the creek. "I can't find him," she sobbed. "He was right beside me. He was right here."

Rusty stumbled through the current, bellowing over the roar of rain. "The tiger's loose! Someone get a rope!"

Stetson's voice cut through, hard and commanding. "Margie's pinned — Abe, help me move this beam!"

Abe lurched forward, dragging his leg like dead weight. He found Margie crushed beneath warped metal, her arm twisted, her face streaked with blood. Pain tore through him, but he set his massive hands beneath the wreckage. His muscles screamed as he lifted. "Damn, it's heavy…"

Stetson dropped beside him, heaving, straining. Together they shifted enough for Margie to drag herself free, shrieking in pain. Abe collapsed back into the mud, clutching his leg. Something inside had snapped. Broken. Useless.

Bobo floated past, face down. Stetson pulled him in, slapping his cheeks. "Come on, Rubber Boy. Bounce back. That's your trick, remember?" But the body was limp. The ringmaster's face fell as he let go. The creek carried Bobo away. Then, through the sheets of rain, a flicker of light pulsed against the trees. Blue. Unmistakable. A police car was pulling up to the scene, its siren lost in the howl of the storm.

Sally and Ally sobbed in the water, one of their arms bent at a sickening angle. But Priscilla wasn't listening.

"Matty Matty!" she cried, her voice raw, breaking. She stumbled onto a rock, her body silhouetted against a flash of lightning. Her eyes locked on the dark trees rising beyond the creek.

"He's out there," she whispered, voice trembling with conviction. "He has to be. Please… help me look."

Abe tried to rise, his massive body shaking. "My leg…" he groaned, collapsing back onto the creekbed.

"Spread out!" Stetson barked. "We'll find him!"

And then, through the storm, it came.

A sound.

A bleat.

Ally froze, her lips quivering. "Did you hear that?"

Out of the treeline, a rookie officer in his 20s, Wendell Hodges, rushed toward the wreck, his face pale as he surveyed the carnage.

"Oh my God!"

He spotted Abe struggling in the mud and helped drag him to the relative safety of the creekbed. As

Hodges sized up the giant of a man, his eyes caught on the other survivors — a bearded lady, conjoined twins — and he did a double take, his mind struggling to process the scene.

"Is... is everyone alive?"

Stetson shook his head grimly. "We lost one." He glanced downstream, where Bobo's limp body was washed up against a fallen tree. "We're looking for a little boy!"

Hodges ran a hand through his soaked hair. "I'll radio for backup. Be right back!" He turned and rushed back into the treeline toward the road where his cruiser was parked.

Still in the creek, Willie gripped a half-submerged trunk, scanning the trees, his small body shivering with cold. "Matthew! You yell back, you hear me?" His voice broke into nothing.

No answer.

Priscilla dropped to her knees in the torrent, clawing at the rocky creekbed with bare hands as her sobs rose into the storm. "Where is he?" Her voice cracked, swallowed by the rush of the creek.

Downstream, beyond the chaos of the wreck, the goats were watching. They stood at the tree line, half-shrouded in shadow, their eyes glinting faintly in the broken light. Six of them, mangy and wild-eyed, their coats slick with rain. They watched with unnerving stillness, like sentinels called from the woods themselves.

On the far bank, half-buried in mud and washed-up branches, Matthew lay motionless. His small body was a sodden heap, his Raggedy Andy doll clutched limply to his chest. For a moment he seemed lifeless.

Then one of the goats stepped forward, nudging

him with its muzzle. Another butted gently at his side, pressing its head beneath his limp arm.

Matthew stirred. A cough rattled out of him, weak but alive. His eyes fluttered open. Blinking, dazed, he pushed himself upright. Mud streaked his hair. His lips trembled as he tried to catch his breath.

The goats stood in a loose half-circle around him, their ragged outlines cutting against the pale drizzle. Observing. Studying.

Somewhere in the distance came the faint, muffled cry of his mother. "Matthew!"

He didn't turn. Didn't react. Blood trickled in a thin line from behind his ear, seeping into the collar of his shirt. He could not hear her.

Instead, his eyes followed the lead goat as it turned and began walking slowly into the woods. At the tree line it paused, glancing back with a stillness that felt almost human.

Matthew rose unsteadily to his feet, his small legs trembling beneath him. Cold and alone in the drizzle, he shivered as he took a hesitant step forward. Drawn by the strange animals, he began to limp after them, following their swaying backs as they moved through the brush in single file. Step by step, he trailed the goats into the Kentucky hills, deeper and deeper into the waiting woods. The herd pressed on until they reached an opening in a great rock formation, slipping inside one by one. Matthew paused only a moment before limping after them, vanishing into the stone's dark mouth.

By morning, the wreck was a crime scene. Mist clung to the ground, thick and heavy, as Hodges and another officer in slickers picked through the twisted train cars. Officers scribbled notes, workers shifted mangled metal beams, the air heavy with smoke, mud and silence.

Rusty stumbled past, his face drawn and gray, mud plastered to his clothes. A rope was looped tight around the neck of the circus tiger, the beast pacing and snarling, its fur dripping. Two officers strained to keep it steady as Rusty held the line with raw, rope-burned hands.

A patrol car pulled up, tires crunching on gravel. Chief Don Green stepped out, firm in his movements but grave in his expression. He stopped at the edge of the wreck, eyes sweeping the ruin, absorbing it all — the shattered cars, the bodies, the haunted faces of the survivors.

The silence of the morning was broken only by the hiss of cooling steel and the faint buzz of cicadas, rising like a dirge.

Survivors sat scattered across the scene like fragments of the wreck itself. Beneath a sprawling oak, Abe leaned back against the trunk, his enormous frame broken and humbled. His leg was bound in a crude splint of rope and planks, the effort of breathing etched deep into his face. Beside him, Margie nursed a tin cup of coffee with her good hand, the other swaddled in stiff bandages. Neither spoke. Their silence was as loud as the wreck behind them.

Just a few feet away, a large white sheet lay over Bobo's body. Dark blotches of crimson seeped through where the cuts had been, stark against the pale fabric.

Abe and Margie tried not to look, but their eyes betrayed them, flicking toward the covered remains of their friend again and again. Margie bit her lip, doing her best not to cry. Abe lowered his head into his large hands trying to hide his tears.

Chief Don Green stood at the edge of the woods, boots sunk in wet earth, voice cutting across the wreck like a whip. "Let's go! Fan out! Ten feet between you! We find the boy today, you hear me?!"

Stetson echoed him, his ringmaster's tone now stripped of flair, urgent and raw. "You heard him! Go!"

Priscilla shoved through the underbrush, her skirts torn and plastered to her legs. She called out until her throat was hoarse, every cry breaking in the trees. "Matthew! Baby! It's Momma!"

Willie, mud-caked and limping but unyielding, scoured the base of a fallen trunk. His voice cracked when he shouted, "Matthew! Say something—we're right here!"

"Matty Matty!" Priscilla's voice rose to a wail. "Where are you?!"

Others joined in, their calls fading into the vast quiet of the Kentucky hills. Sally and Ally trudged past, one arm bound in a sling. They paused often, listening, but nothing answered.

On the creek bank, Stetson moved like a man possessed, his sharp eyes raking the ground, searching for tracks, for anything.

"Nothing back there, Chief," an officer called from deeper in the woods.

"No sign of him on the far side either," another added. "We've got dogs coming in from Jefferson County," someone shouted, "but it'll be a few hours before they get here."

By late afternoon, hope sagged beneath exhaustion. The survivors moved like ghosts through the mud, soaked in sweat and loss. Priscilla's face was pale, her hands trembling as she clutched the soaked fabric of her dress. Willie walked beside her, silent, his teeth clinched tight as stone.

Chief Green approached slowly, his hat in his hands. "Ma'am. Sir." He swallowed. "We're going to suspend the search for the night."

Priscilla's voice broke in a shriek. "No... please— no. He's just a little boy."

Green's face was grim. "We'll pick it up again at first light." He turned to Officer Hodges. "Have the creek dragged. Start at the bend by that big oak over there."

Hodges nodded and swiftly made his way into the treeline.

Priscilla's head snapped toward the police chief. "No!" Her knees gave way, and she collapsed in the mud, sobbing.

Willie caught her, wrapping his small, strong arms around her body as she shook against him. His own eyes glistened, though he tried to hide it. "He's out here somewhere," he whispered fiercely. "I know it. I know it."

Stetson crouched beside them, his usual grin absent, his hand heavy on Willie's shoulder. "We'll keep looking," he promised, his voice low, solemn. "Whatever it takes."

Sally and Ally came forward quietly, one draping an arm across Priscilla's trembling back. Abe limped toward them, dragging his broken leg, and folded one massive arm across the huddle. Together, the troupe held to each other, bound by grief and desperation.

Above them, a tattered circus banner — its letters faded, its edges torn — flapped weakly in the breeze. *SEE THE WONDERS!* it read, snagged cruelly in the branches of a broken tree.

The hills rolled away in silence.

As the sun began to set, its weak light spilled over the devastation. The wreck lay in ruins, twisted steel and shattered cars strewn across the banks like bones. At the center, the dead locomotive sat blackened and bent, its iron frame jutting from the mud like the carcass of some extinct creature.

The scene held, quiet and merciless, as if the land itself had swallowed the boy whole.

◆ ◆ ◆ ◆ ◆ ◆

BACK TO PRESENT

The memory seemed to drain Abe as much as the accident itself had all those years ago. He rubbed the corner of his eye with a thick, unsteady hand, composing himself before speaking.

"My friend Bobo was killed that night," he said at last. His voice was quieter now, almost fragile. "He was a good man."

Shelley leaned in, wrapping her arms around her grandfather. For a moment, he let her hold him. Then he exhaled sharply, forcing the grief back down into the well where it had lived for forty years.

"So that's why you stayed here in Louisville," she whispered.

Abe gave a humorless smile. "Snapped my leg like a twig. Couldn't stand the damn cast. Couldn't stand the thought of another train either. Got work in the kitchen at the Seelbach. That's where I met your grandma." He paused, the weight of it pressing on his shoulders. "Never went back to the show."

Shelley hesitated before leaning closer, her voice dropping to a hush. "So that rumor… that something escaped from the train that night."

Abe shifted in his chair. The tip of his cane tapped lightly against the linoleum, steady as a clock. He didn't look at her, only out the window, where the morning light spread across the courtyard.

"The tiger did get loose," he said finally. "That part's true. But Rusty and some of the officers caught it the next morning." His jaw tightened. "The only one we never found was Matthew. Willie and Priscilla's little boy."

The room went very still. Shelley and Jimmy exchanged a glance.

"You think he's still out there?" she asked, her words trembling just above a whisper.

Abe didn't answer right away. His eyes stayed fixed on the horizon as if he could see beyond the glass, past the courtyard and the hedges, into the Kentucky hills where the train had gone down.

"I try to forget," he muttered. "All of it."

He motioned at Jimmy's phone without looking. Jimmy obeyed, tucking it away. The quiet grew heavier, thick as smoke.

"The wreck happened," Abe said at last. His voice was low, measured, as if he were laying down stone. "That much I can tell you." He let the silence stretch before adding, firmer now, "But monsters? No. There ain't no monster out there."

He leaned back, eyes drifting once more to the horizon. His expression was blank, a mask carved by years of trying not to remember.

Shelley and Jimmy sat in the hush that followed, the gravity of his words pressing against them.

The Police Car in the Driveway

The old Chevy truck rattled to a stop on the gravel road, its bumper plastered with faded Kentucky Wildcats stickers. Arnold Summers climbed out, camouflage pants, boots heavy against the earth. From the truck bed he pulled out a hunting rifle, slung it over his shoulder, and set off toward the tree line. A weathered *NO TRESPASSING* sign leaned drunkenly to one side. Strips of yellowed police tape clung to the brush like cobwebs, snapping weakly in the breeze as Arnold ducked beneath and pushed on.

The woods swallowed him. Quiet pressed in on all sides. Each step sank into damp soil, his boots crunching over the occasional brittle leaf. A rock outcropping jutted from a rise in the earth ahead, half-concealed by brush and branches. Arnold slowed, eyes narrowing. For a moment, the fallen limbs seemed unnatural, possibly placed. He took two steps closer—then froze.

Something was watching.

The faintest bleat broke the silence. He spun, heart hammering, only to find nothing. No eyes in the dusk. No figure between the trees. The woods breathed around him, empty. He licked his lips, muttered under his breath, and moved on.

Higher ground rose ahead. As Arnold climbed, pushing through brambles that clung to his fatigues, the trestle emerged—a black iron scar across the horizon, silhouetted against the dying light.

At the top, he paused on the rail bed, chest heaving. The last of the day's sun stretched long, blood-red shadows through the trees. A goat bleated again.

Close. His knuckles whitened around the rifle's stock.

"What was that?" he whispered to no one.

The woods offered only silence.

Arnold started forward, boots striking the warped wooden ties of the track. The wind grew stronger, whistling through the iron supports. Beneath him the creek murmured faintly, far too far below. He was halfway across when movement caught his eye—two goats, shaggy and wild, slipping into the undergrowth. Their presence made the hair on his arms rise.

Then came the whistle.

It was faint at first, carried on the wind, then building—a low, mournful wail that froze him in place. Arnold whipped around.

A headlight burst through the dusk, a burning star on steel rails.

"Damnit…"

He turned and sprinted back across the ties, rifle banging against his shoulder, boots slamming wood. The whistle screamed. The trestle shuddered with the weight of the oncoming engine.

Then he saw it.

Something stepped out from the dark ahead, tall, black, massive. It blocked the span with an ease that seemed deliberate, as though it had been waiting.

Arnold stopped dead. His breath came fast, too fast. The rifle jerked up.

"What the hell…" His voice cracked against the wind.

The shape shifted.

One impossibly long arm swung out.

The blow came with inhuman force.

Arnold left his feet, flung sideways like a ragdoll.

He fell — air rushing past, rifle spinning free — until the ground rose up to meet him with a wet, cracking thud.

He lay twisted in the mud, eyes wide, glassy, mouth frozen mid-breath.

Above, the train roared across the trestle, thunder on iron. Its rumble seemed to wake the woods, but what answered was not the cry of any beast Arnold knew.

A sound rose up in its wake, a cross between a bleat and a growl.

It echoed through the Kentucky trees as the black form melted back into the forest, gone as quickly as it had come.

◆ ◆ ◆ ◆ ◆ ◆

The following morning, mist hung heavy over the Pope Lick woods, curling low around the trestle that carved its way across the sky. The iron span loomed above, black against the pale gray morning. Birds trilled faintly, their songs muted as if even they knew better than to linger here.

Randy Hawkins followed a narrow deer path through the brush, his boots caked in mud, a GoPro strapped to his chest. He spoke in the casual, half-mocking cadence of a man who wanted to sound brave on camera.

"So this is it," he muttered, swinging the lens toward the trestle. "The infamous Pope Lick trestle. Creepy as hell out here."

The words barely left his mouth when something caught his eye. A shape in the weeds near one of the trestle's support beams. Randy froze. His stomach dropped.

"Oh, God..."

He pushed closer through the undergrowth and stopped cold.

A body.

The man lay crumpled beneath the steel column, limbs twisted unnaturally, one boot gone. A faint trail of blood streaked through the grass back toward the base of the trestle, as if he had tried to crawl before giving out. His face was hidden, but the finality of it was undeniable.

Randy's breath rattled. His hands trembled as he fumbled his phone from his pocket.

"Sir... Sir, can you hear me?" His voice broke into a whisper. He already knew the answer.

He dialed with shaking fingers, eyes fixed on the corpse.

Somewhere beyond the trees, something moved. Quiet, patient. Watching.

An hour later, the place was swarming with police. Yellow tape flapped weakly between the trees as officers spread out beneath the trestle. Radios crackled. A coroner's van idled, its back doors yawning open, ready.

The body lay beneath a sheet now, stark white against the wet ground. A hunting rifle rested in the grass just a few feet away, its barrel muddy.

Officer Cole stood stiffly nearby, his eyes locked on the sheet. He said nothing as another officer crouched to snap photographs, the shutter clicking in sharp bursts that seemed to cut through the morning air.

A detective closed his notebook, lips pressed thin, then looked up at Cole. "The deceased is Arnold Summers." His voice was low but final.

"Go tell the family."

Cole swallowed hard. The mist swirled around his

boots as he turned away.

Above, the trestle groaned in the wind.

♦ ♦ ♦ ♦ ♦ ♦

Clouds drifted overhead, their shadows crawling across the quiet neighborhood. A police cruiser turned slowly into the Summers' gravel driveway, tires crunching on the stones. The house stood still, curtains drawn against the morning light, as if it already knew what was coming.

A knock at the door.

Sandra opened the front door halfway, a dish towel clutched in her hands. She was still wiping them absently when she saw the uniform. The towel slipped from her grasp and landed without a sound on the porch. Her hand rose to her mouth. Her eyes filled before a word was spoken.

Behind her, Barry stepped into the doorway. His eyes followed hers, landing on Officer Cole, who stood stiffly at the foot of the porch. Barry's knees seemed to weaken all at once.

"No..." His voice cracked. He staggered forward a step, shaking his head as though denial alone could stop the moment. His face crumpled, tears streaking down before he could wipe them away. "Arnold?"

Officer Cole's eyes lowered. He gave a single, heavy nod.

"I'm sorry, sir." His voice was steady but quiet, the words almost lost to the stillness of the morning.

Sandra broke then, a sob ripping through her chest as she clutched Barry. Barry stood rigid, frozen in the doorway, while his wife wrapped her arms around him, pulling him into her grief. His hands hovered for a moment, empty, before he finally let them fall around her, holding on because there was nothing else left to do.

The house behind them was silent, the world holding its breath. Only the clouds moved, drifting slowly past, indifferent to the poor family who had just lost another loved one.

◆ ◆ ◆ ◆ ◆ ◆

Muted evening light filtered through the half-closed blinds, striping the Summers' living room in pale shadows. A box of tissues sat abandoned on the coffee table beside a mug of tea. Sandra and Barry were on the couch, their bodies drawn inward—Sandra's eyes raw and swollen, her hands clamped around her knees, Barry staring at the floor as if it might open and swallow him.

The front door creaked. Jimmy stepped inside, his backpack slung over one shoulder, his voice casual, even eager.

"Dad, I need some help with my biology…"

The words died when he saw them. The air in the room was heavy, stifling. He let his backpack slip to the floor with a soft thud.

Sandra's voice was barely a whisper. "Jimmy… sit down."

He hesitated, searching their faces. "Mom… what's going on?"

"Please," she urged, her hand trembling in her lap.

Jimmy crossed the room slowly and dropped into the armchair across from them. The silence pressed down. The only sound was the steady tick of the wall clock, louder than it had ever seemed before. Barry shifted, then looked to Sandra. Sandra looked back. Neither spoke. Jimmy felt his chest tighten. Something was wrong. Really wrong.

Sandra's lips quivered before the words slipped out. "It's your uncle, honey..."

Barry's voice followed, thick and breaking. "He went out into the woods. Looking for... whatever got John."

Jimmy's jaw dropped. The weight of it hit him all at once. He couldn't breathe. Couldn't think. He shot to his feet, eyes wet, and stumbled down the hall to his room.

He slammed the door, collapsed on the edge of his bed, and fumbled for the remote. The TV blinked on, filling the room with a bluish glow.

WLKL-13 NEWS flashed across the screen. Drone footage hovered over the Pope Lick trestle, the skeletal structure cutting across the canopy of dense Kentucky woods. The headline crawled across the bottom:

BODY FOUND BENEATH POPE LICK TRESTLE – THIRD DEATH THIS WEEK

Trey Robertson sat at the news desk, tie askew, his voice steady but grim.

"This morning, a hiker discovered the body of forty-three-year-old Arnold Summers directly beneath the Pope Lick trestle. Authorities say the position of the body and extensive blunt force trauma suggest he fell from the top of the structure."

The broadcast cut to flashing police lights behind a curtain of yellow tape. Fog clung to the trees. Forensic tents stood at the base of the trestle. A white sheet was lifted into a body bag.

Jimmy dragged a hand through his hair, the room

spinning. His phone buzzed against the bedspread — a text from Shelley:

OMG! Is that your uncle?

He let the phone fall from his hand, its screen dimming as it slipped into silence. Jimmy leaned back against the wall, eyes brimming, staring blankly at the TV. His world had cracked wide open, and he was left in the hollow center of it, trying to comprehend how fast everything had fallen apart.

Across the river in New Albany, the glow of a television filled a modest room at Willow Glen Retirement Home. A framed photo of a young Shelley smiled from the nightstand, the only hint of warmth against the pale walls. The rest of the room was still, save for the faint hum of the television.

Abe sat hunched in his chair, his cane leaning against his leg like a sentinel. On the coffee table before him sat the small bowl of M&Ms. He plucked a few out, the candies rattling softly against the glass, and tossed them into his mouth without thought. His eyes never left the screen.

The anchors spoke in hushed, practiced tones about Arnold Summers — the third death at the Pope Lick trestle in a single week. The footage rolled again, the skeletal span cutting across the Kentucky woods, wrapped in police tape and fog.

The shifting light from the screen flickered across Abe's weathered face, sharpening the lines around his mouth and eyes. His jaw worked slowly, hardening with each second that passed. He reached for the remote, his hand trembling, and pressed rewind.

The drone footage replayed, silently this time, the trestle looming across the gray woods. Abe didn't blink. His gnarled fingers tightened around the armrest of his chair until the knuckles whitened. His breath came shorter, shallower, as if something unseen had crawled back out of the dark memories he had spent forty years trying to bury.

Ashes to Ashes

The next day, the sky was pale and cloudless, the kind of washed-out day that made grief feel heavier. Barry stood beside Sandra and Jimmy as the gravediggers shoveled earth onto the modest coffin. Each dull thud of dirt struck like a blow. Jimmy brushed at his cheek, trying to hide the tears. Sandra reached for Barry's hand, squeezing tight. He swallowed hard, fighting the sob rising in his throat.

The preacher's voice carried softly over the small gathering, words worn thin from centuries of repetition—*ashes to ashes, dust to dust.* Heads bowed, the prayer falling into silence.

From the corner of his eye, Jimmy saw movement. Shelley, dressed in a simple black dress, stepped forward just as the preacher offered the final "Amen." Her eyes met Jimmy's, a sad smile flickering across her face. Jimmy gave the smallest of nods in return. Then she drifted away, her figure thinning into the crowd.

Sandra slipped her arms around Jimmy's shoulders, murmuring, "Are you alright, honey?"

Jimmy nodded, though his voice cracked. "Yeah, Mom. Just… a little sad."

As his mother doted on him, Jimmy's eyes wandered across the cemetery. A few feet away, John's grave sat raw and unsettled, the earth still dark and fresh, no stone yet to mark it. The sight hollowed him.

Barry and Sandra walked with Jimmy to stand at the foot of that grave. Together they looked down into the bare patch of soil, their arms curling protectively around their son. The three of them stood there in silence, bound in grief, staring at the place where John now lay.

◆ ◆ ◆ ◆ ◆ ◆

That night the house was silent. In his room, Jimmy sat cross-legged on the bed, the only light the soft glow of his phone. His eyes were raw and swollen from crying, his thumb moving slowly over the glass as he scrolled through memories.

John's face filled the screen again and again. Christmas morning—both of them in flannel pajamas, laughing through piles of shredded red and green wrapping paper. Summer at the pool—John mid-air in a cannonball, arms tucked to his knees, frozen in sunlight and chaos. Each image pressed against Jimmy's chest like a bruise.

He stopped on a video and pressed play.

On the screen, John bounced a basketball in the driveway, looking like a pro in his Kentucky Wildcats jersey and basketball shorts. Facing off against him was Barry, dressed in a plain white t-shirt, black shorts that were too tight for a man in his forties, and white socks pulled all the way up to his knees.

John laughed, pointing a finger at his dad. "Looking good, old man! Real dorky."

"Just because you're dressed like a basketball player don't make you one," His father sneered back, getting into a low stance.

From behind the camera, Jimmy's younger voice could be heard giggling. "I got next, Dad!"

"Old man?" Barry sneered… "Oh, I'll show you a thing or two…"

Chuckling, John slipped past him with ease—a

quick crossover, a spin, and a soft layup. Instead of just running back, John did a ridiculous moonwalk in the middle of the driveway as Barry pouted and mumbled under his breath just behind him. John turned straight to the camera, still gliding backward, pointing to the camera.

"That's for you, Jimmy," he said, and then blew a kiss to the camera and laughed.

The sound of his brother's voice gutted him. Jimmy clamped his lips together, fighting the sob rising up. He wiped at his eyes with his palm and set the phone down, this time on a small tripod pointed at his desk.

He pulled the chair out and sat stiffly, legs crossed, trying to look composed though his chest shook slightly. A long pause, his thumb hovering over the record button. His eyes drifted to the subscriber count just below it: 528. It had been 202 just a few days ago. More than double. For a fraction of a second, a flicker of intrigue cut through the sorrow; he was slightly impressed. He pushed the feeling away, took a deep breath, and then he hit record.

"This has been a rough week," he began, voice hoarse. He swallowed, forcing a breath. "As many of you know... that thing in the woods killed my brother." His throat tightened, but he pushed on. "My uncle got drunk and thought he'd go out there looking for it. Well..." He broke off, blinking, jaw clenched. "It... it found him first."

He sat in silence for a beat, the camera's red light glaring back at him. Then his voice steadied, low but sure. "I'm going to get to the bottom of it. For John. For Uncle Arnold."

Another pause. His eyes locked with the lens, unblinking, as though daring the thing in the woods to listen.

Then he reached forward. The red light clicked off. Jimmy sighed. The room went still again.

◆ ◆ ◆ ◆ ◆ ◆

Moonlight spilled through a broken canopy of bare autumn trees, silvering the ridge above the river. A deer stepped cautiously from the treeline, its ears twitching, nostrils flaring. The forest was too quiet. No crickets. No owls. Nothing.

A sharp SNAP of a twig shattered the silence.

The deer bolted — too late.

Something black surged from the brush, crawling and charging in the same motion, its shape a blur between human and beast. In a single bound it was upon the deer. A sickening crack of bone echoed through the trees, then silence.

Minutes later, the limp carcass was dragged through wet leaves, leaving a crimson trail across the earth. The trail led to a ridge, to a rock formation obscured by brush and limbs. Inside it was littered with scattered animal bones, half-eaten carcasses, and scraps of old circus debris.

Inside, moonlight filtered weakly through holes in the rocks. A cracked funhouse mirror leaned against the wall. Nearby, a mold-flecked poster of *Stetson Sterling's World of Wonders* sagged against the stone, the faded print obscured by childish scribbles. And in the corner, half-buried in dirt, lay a dirty Raggedy Andy doll, one eye missing.

The creature released its prize. Blood pooled beneath the deer's neck as the black form crouched low.

From the shadows, several goats emerged. They circled carefully, bowing their heads, silent in reverence.

The figure squatted among them — the alpha.

He tore into the deer's throat with gnashing teeth. The goats settled close around him, guardians of their king.

The woods made no sound but the slow, wet rip of flesh being devoured.

◆ ◆ ◆ ◆ ◆ ◆

GOATMAN LIVES?

The office was small and suffocating, clutter stacked in the corners and a single fluorescent bulb buzzing overhead. On the whiteboard someone had scrawled in black marker: **GOATMAN??** The question hung there like a dare, absurd yet unsettling.

Chief Hodges sat behind his desk, staring at his monitor. He leaned forward, elbows braced, eyes narrowed at the shaky footage pulled from evidence — Randy Hawkins' GoPro, recovered after Arnold Summers' body was found under the trestle.

The video wobbled as Randy hiked through the woods, his voice a faint nervous narration. Branches swayed. Fog shifted. Then — something.

Hodges froze. Rewound. Played it again. There, just beyond the trees: a shape. Tall. Dark. Motionless.

His thumb hesitated over the spacebar. He zoomed in until the pixels smeared into gray blur. The outline became clearer, if not less impossible — something massive, hunched at the edges, watching from the mist. Just standing there. Just watching.

A cold prickle ran down Hodges' neck. His hand tightened on the mouse. He whispered under his breath, the words more for himself than anyone else.

"What is that?"

He grabbed the radio, thumb pressing the call button, his eyes never leaving the figure frozen on the screen.

"Cole... I need you in my office. Now."

The radio crackled a faint acknowledgment, but Hodges hardly heard it. He stayed locked on the image, the blurred silhouette in the fog. And for a long moment, he swore the thing on the screen was staring right back at him.

A moment later, Officer Cole stepped inside, his eyes immediately drawn to the large monitor on Hodges' desk. "What are you looking at, Chief?"

Hodges didn't look away from the frozen image. He tapped a thick finger against the screen. "You see that? There's something out there."

Cole leaned in, squinting at the grainy footage of the fog-shrouded trees. "I don't see it, sir." He moved closer, his nose nearly touching the screen, his eyes tracing the outlines of the branches. "Oh!" His eyes bulged, his professional calm shattering for a second. "What is that?"

Hodges leaned back in his chair, the movement heavy with exhaustion. He let out a slow breath, a chill crawling up his spine that had nothing to do with the temperature in the room.

◆ ◆ ◆ ◆ ◆ ◆

The hallway of Eastern High was a blur of movement—lockers slamming, voices overlapping and shoes squeaking on the vinyl tiling. Posters for homecoming and ACT prep flapped loose on the bulletin board, half-torn at the corners. Jimmy moved through it all like a ghost, hoodie up, headphones hanging slack around his neck. He kept his eyes on the floor, avoiding the stares, the whispers.

He stopped at his locker, spinning the dial with a dull rhythm, when a voice cut through the noise.

"Hey."

He turned. Shelley stood there, close enough that her words were almost lost in the chaos, her phone raised like a secret. On the screen, a video played — big bold text across the thumbnail: **GOATMAN LIVES? Kentucky Teens Found Dead – Urban Legend or Real Killer?**

Jimmy's chest tightened. He looked her in the eye.

"You said you wanted answers," Shelley said, her voice low, urgent. "Let's go out there and see if it's really true."

For a moment he just stared at the phone. Then past her, down the crowded hallway where kids shoved and laughed and lived lives that didn't feel broken. He swallowed hard.

"You really wanna go out in the woods?" His voice was flat, but the weight behind it betrayed him. "After everything?"

"I'm not saying we go deep," she replied quickly. "Just... look around. Daylight. We don't have to cross the trestle or anything." She hesitated, then added, almost sheepish as she patted her jacket pocket: "I've got pepper spray."

He didn't answer. Not right away. His fingers lingered on the edge of the locker door, thinking, knuckles white.

"It feels wrong," he said finally. "Going out there and filming... like I'm just trying to get views off what happened to my brother."

Shelley shook her head. "Then don't film. Let's just go for us. For your brother. Your uncle…"

Her words hung there. He closed his eyes for a second, and when he opened them again, something inside had shifted. His shoulders stiffened, a new resolve setting into place.

"No," he said. "If we go out there... if we find something... we put it online. They can't ignore it. We can make them listen."

He turned to her fully now, meeting her gaze with a determination she hadn't seen in him before.

"Let's do it."

She studied him—this boy who, only days ago, was just another kid chasing views online. Now, the grief had carved something harder, sharper into him. Shelley gave a small nod, her voice soft but steady.

"I'll pick you up after school."

Livestream

Two hours later, the woods near Pope Lick were hushed beneath the dying light. Shadows stretched long between the trunks, swallowing the trail in an uneasy half-dark. Every sound — every crackle of leaves, every rustle of wind — felt amplified, like the forest itself was holding its breath.

Jimmy followed just behind Shelley as she pushed through the overgrown path, weeds and dead branches clawing at their legs. She gripped a small canister of pepper spray so tightly her knuckles had gone pale. Jimmy's eyes kept darting between the trees, searching for movement, while in his other hand his phone glowed.

The screen showed *1,202 viewers... climbing fast.*

"I think this is it," Shelley whispered. "The old service path. It should lead right up to the tracks."

Jimmy glanced upward, past the tree line. The silhouette of the trestle loomed ahead, black against the orange smear of the fading sky. He swallowed hard. "Yeah," he said. "There it is."

At the base of the iron structure, Jimmy stopped. The trestle rose over them like some vast skeleton, each beam silhouetted against the dusk. He lowered his phone, suddenly unsure if he even wanted to keep filming.

"You good?" Shelley asked, watching him.

He nodded, but quieter, he admitted, "Yeah. Just... weird being here. In real life. You know?"

She tilted her head. "What made you start your channel anyway? The whole J Summertime thing?"

A faint smirk tugged at his mouth. "When I was

fourteen. Just messing around. Dumb jokes. Fireworks in the backyard." He paused, staring up at the towering iron. His voice grew heavier. "It's gotten darker since then. And with John... with my uncle... I thought about shutting it down. Felt like I was just feeding the same beast that killed them."

His hand tightened around the phone. "But this thing in the woods... it's blown up. Biggest thing I've ever done. And I realized all those people watching? It feels like they're waiting to see it through."

His eyes stayed fixed on the trestle as he breathed in, hardening. "I have to see it through. For John. For Uncle Arnold."

Shelley watched him silently, the look in his eyes different now — no longer about followers, but about a purpose.

Jimmy tapped the screen again. The red light blinked to life.

"Going live at Pope Lick Park," he murmured. "Showtime."

1,112 viewers.

Minutes later, their boots echoed against the trestle's wooden slats. Shelley went first, stepping cautiously, arms out slightly for balance. Jimmy followed, keeping his eyes fixed straight ahead but still catching flashes of the dizzying drop in his periphery.

"Just don't look down," Shelley muttered.

"Too late," Jimmy said through clenched teeth.

Then her foot slipped. She lurched sideways, grabbing his arm for balance. Her phone tumbled from her grip, clattering against the wood before disappearing through a gap.

"Dammit," she hissed. "I've only had that phone a

week or two. My mom's going to kill me." She leaned over the edge, squinting into the dimming woods. "Do you see it?"

Jimmy scanned below, but the undergrowth swallowed everything in shadow. "I don't think so."

He slid his own phone into his pocket. "Come on. We can find it. Should be right below us." He pointed toward the dark trees beneath the trestle. "Somewhere down there."

They left the rail bed and climbed down the slope beneath the trestle. Holding onto each other, they slipped on loose dirt, grabbing at roots for balance. The woods were already sinking into dusk, the shadows thickening as they picked their way through weeds and tall grass. Jimmy brushed aside leaves, scanning the ground for Shelley's phone. She moved ahead with her pepper spray clenched tight, frustration sharp in her voice.

"It's gotta be here somewhere."

"We'll find it," Jimmy said, though his own eyes kept darting nervously toward a rock formation obscured by brush. "Just keep looking."

The trestle loomed menacingly above them.

Then it came—a sound that made both of them freeze. A bleat, but wrong. Distorted. Half-human. It drifted through the trees like a curse.

Jimmy spun around, "Is that a goat?"

"That… didn't sound like a goat," Shelley whispered.

Jimmy straightened, jaw tight. "Let's move."

They began backing away, their steps quick, shallow. Branches snapped. Brush rustled. And then it rose.

Through a clearing thirty yards away, a shape

unfolded from a crouch and kept unfolding until it towered over six feet. Its body was a tangled coat of matted hair and leaves, its posture a warped imitation of man and beast both. Long, sinewy arms hung low, hands dangling. Its head tilted, and two eyes—dark, glistening, intelligent—locked on them.

A guttural rumble shook its chest, a sound halfway between a growl and a goat's bleat. Yellowed teeth caught the last shred of light.

Shelley screamed. Jimmy moved towards her. "Go!"

But the thing was faster. It lunged, slamming into him and driving him to the dirt. Claws raked at his chest. Teeth snapped inches from his face. Jimmy strained against its weight, muscles screaming. "Get off me!"

Shelley fumbled with her pepper spray, panic freezing her hand. She couldn't aim with Jimmy thrashing beneath it. The creature forced his head back, its jaws yawning wide over his exposed throat.

"Stop!" she screamed.

It didn't.

"Stop, Matthew!"

The name cut the air like a blade.

The beast froze. Slowly, its head turned. Its dark eyes fixed on Shelley.

"Matty Matty…" Her voice shook, but she didn't back away.

The creature tilted its head, studying her, nostrils flaring as if it remembered. Jimmy coughed, straining to push himself upright. The thing shifted its weight, rising from Jimmy, taking one deliberate step toward her. Shelley began to backpedal and tripped.

Gunfire split the air. POP! POP!

The creature reared back with a snarl, then vanished into the woods on all fours, faster than anything human had a right to be.

Three figures burst from the brush, guns drawn, uniforms flashing in the dim light. Officer Cole in the lead, his face hard, followed by Stark and Morales, rifles raised.

"We made contact!" Cole barked into his radio. "It's fleeing east."

Jimmy staggered upright, blood streaking his forehead. He pulled Shelley to her feet. Both of them were trembling, the shock still setting in. Cole lowered his gun, glaring.

"What the hell are you two doing out here?"

Jimmy tried to speak, his voice cracking. "We were just trying to figure out what happened. Her grandpa…"

Cole cut him off with a sharp shake of his head. "This area's been cordoned off for a reason."

Stark, still scanning the trees, growled, "We're going after it."

Cole nodded. "Alright. I've got them. Go."

The two officers disappeared into the brush, swallowed by the dark. Cole turned back, his gaze dropping to Jimmy's bleeding face.

"You're lucky someone flagged your livestream," he said grimly. "Otherwise…"

Jimmy hung his head, refusing to look the officer in the eye.

Cole motioned toward the faint glow of patrol car lights deeper in the trees. "Come on. Let's get you out of here."

Cole marched Jimmy and Shelley back toward the police car, the trees around them whispering in the wind. The woods seemed to press in closer with every step, their shadows thickening, hiding things just beyond the beam of a flashlight. Behind them, the woods swallowed Stark and Morales whole.

Just past the treeline, the sun had begun to set. Sunlight filtered weakly through the broken canopy, painting orange streaks across moss and rock. The air carried the smell of damp leaves and rain-soaked earth. Crickets had begun their chorus, sharp and uneven, as though warning of something they could sense but not see.

Stark trudged ahead, heavy boots crushing damp leaves. Morales followed close, flashlight beam jerking with each step. They ducked under low-hanging limbs and climbed over a fallen pine slick with moss, then stopped.

"You sure it went this way?" Stark muttered, breath fogging in the cool night air. "Damn it. This is that same rock formation. We've circled back to where those kids were."

Morales pointed his beam at the ground where mud and leaves were torn into ragged impressions. "Something tore through here. Big. Almost like footprints."

Stark grunted. "Keep your finger off the trigger till you're sure. Last thing I need is friendly fire in a cryptid hunt."

They dropped down into a shallow ravine, vines clawing at their arms. On the far side, half-hidden behind twisted roots and bramble, gaped a narrow black opening in a rock formation.

From within came a bleat. Warped. Guttural. Wrong.

Morales froze. "That… didn't sound right."

Stark's voice was a low rasp. "Flashlights out. Guns up."

Both men flicked on their beams and stepped into the mouth of the cave.

The air turned damp, reeking of mold and iron. Roots hung from the ceiling like veins, dripping slow rivulets of water. As their lights swept across the den, the beams suddenly struck a cracked funhouse mirror propped against one wall, scattering the light in a dizzying flash. For a moment, their own reflections stared back, warped and monstrous, before their lights danced away across crude walls gouged out of dirt and stone.

The beam caught a mangled deer carcass collapsed in one corner, its ribs chewed clean, hide peeled away like wet paper. Next to it sat a Raggedy Andy doll—filthy, waterlogged, its remaining eye staring glassy and pale. Around it were scattered children's toys, twigs tied with faded ribbons, and bones stacked like offerings.

Morales crouched, shining his light over the doll. His lip curled. "What the hell is this place?"

Stark didn't kneel. He kept his gun raised, flashlight sweeping over the dark corners. "This ain't no animal," he muttered.

Something wet struck Morales's hand. A heavy drop. He glanced at it, smearing the dark smear with his thumb. For an instant he thought it water until instinct told him otherwise.

He tilted his head up.

The blackness above came alive.

The creature dropped from the ceiling in silence,

hitting with the weight of a boulder. Its claws sank into Morales's skull, slamming his head against the wall. The crunch was wet, final. His flashlight clattered to the ground, beam spinning, strobing across the den in manic flashes of white. For an instant the light caught the creature's face—hair matted and dripping, teeth crooked and brown, eyes burning black.

Stark turned, too slow. "Help!"

The thing lunged, tackling him to the ground. Its jaws opened wide, and with a spray of gore it tore into his throat. Stark's scream choked into a bubbling gasp. Blood splattered across the dirt, pooling against the beam of the fallen flashlight.

Then silence.

The creature crouched over what remained of Officer Stark, tearing, chewing, the sound wet and deliberate. A faint bleat rumbled in its chest, almost satisfied.

After a long moment, it reached out, lifting a cracked goat skull from the ground. The upper half was fitted like a crown, and the beast pressed it down upon its head.

Slowly, it rose and turned toward the cave mouth.

Outside, the sun had vanished completely. Only the thin silver wash of moonlight lit the trees.

The figure stood there framed in shadow, breath heavy, chest rising and falling. Then, tilting its crowned head back, it let loose a deep, guttural bleat that echoed across the woods, a sound of hunger and claim.

"Start from the Beginning"

The interrogation room was small and windowless, its walls painted a lifeless gray that seemed to drink in every word. The air was stale, heavy with the faint scent of disinfectant and old coffee. A wall clock ticked too loud, carving silence into pieces.

Jimmy sat hunched at the interrogation table, holding his right arm. Scratches carved across his face, dried blood caked at his temple. He looked pale, exhausted, hollowed out. Beside him, Shelley sat rigid, trying to hold herself together, though her trembling hands betrayed her calm facade.

Chief Hodges leaned over them, knuckles pressed into the table. His eyes bore into Shelley, skeptical, unyielding. Behind him, Officer Cole paced slowly, arms crossed, teeth grinding like a man chewing on his own doubts.

"So," Hodges said, voice slow and weighted. "Its name is Matthew?"

Shelley's voice cracked as she answered. "You have to believe me. There was a train that crashed back in the seventies…"

"Start from the beginning," Hodges cut in. "What were you doing out there?"

Her composure faltered, but she forced the words out. "We went looking to get some video of the monster. I… I dropped my phone on the trestle."

Jimmy leaned forward, urgent. "We climbed down to find it. Then it came out of nowhere. On all fours. Moved like an animal—" He shivered at the memory. "But it looked like a man."

Hodges narrowed his eyes. "A man?"

Jimmy's hands came up, animated, desperate. "It had a face. Sort of. But hair everywhere. Long arms. It tackled me like a linebacker. I wrestled with it. God, it was so strong—I couldn't get it off me."

"Did you get any video of it?," The chief inquired. Jimmy shook his head. "No sir, when she lost her phone, I put mine up."

Hodges' gaze shifted to Cole. "You're telling me you saw it too?"

Cole stopped pacing, his expression grim. "It was hairy, tall—muscular. Pushing seven feet, maybe more. Stood on two legs." He hesitated. "At first I thought it was a small bear. But it ran... fast. Too fast."

Hodges sank into a chair, rubbing his temples. "Jesus. Three people dead in a week. Nearly made it five." He turned toward Cole. "We're going to need help on this."

Cole nodded in agreement.

"Where's Stark and Morales?" Hodges asked.

Cole's eyes flicked wide. He bolted for the door, radio already in his hand.

The room fell into a brittle silence. Jimmy stared down at his scraped knuckles. Shelley's eyes stayed on him, her lips parting as if to speak, but no words came.

The door slammed open.

Sandra swept in like a storm, her coat half-buttoned, hair pulled back hastily, eyes frantic and wild. "Jimmy!?" She flew across the room and crushed her son into a trembling embrace.

"What were you thinking?" she cried, her voice breaking with fury and fear. "Sneaking out into those woods... after everything that's happened?"

Jimmy didn't answer. His face stayed blank, too drained to argue. His eyes slid past his mother's shoulder to Shelley, who offered the smallest smile—a fragile thread of connection in the chaos.

Cole reentered, his face grim. Sandra turned to him, gathering herself, her voice thick but steady. "Thank you. For saving my son."

Cole nodded, but his gaze darted toward Hodges.

Sandra's eyes followed, then cut sharp to Shelley. Cold now, firm and unyielding. "Stay away from him."

Shelley's smile faltered, but she didn't flinch. She simply nodded, her eyes steady, almost defiant.

Sandra turned back to Jimmy, her voice soft but commanding. "Let's go."

Jimmy rose slowly. As he passed Shelley, he lingered for the briefest breath. Their eyes met—no words, just a tether neither was ready to sever. Then Sandra's hand clamped onto his arm, leading him out into the night.

Cole's voice filled the silence. "No word on Stark or Morales."

Hodges' brow furrowed, his voice low. "God help us." He looked back to Shelley. "Young lady, you're free to go. But listen to me." His stare was iron. "Stay out of the woods."

Shelley didn't answer. She slipped out the door, the clock ticked on, louder than ever.

The hallway of the police department felt hollow at night, stripped of its daytime bustle. Dispatch chatter leaked faintly from a cracked office door, otherwise silence pressed in, broken only by the steady hum of the overhead lights.

Shelley walked slowly, her shoes echoing across

the tile. She was exhausted, still rattled, her mind replaying the woods, the snarling thing, the gunshots. She just wanted to get home.

Then—she froze.

A tall, familiar figure sat in a plastic chair near the front desk, a crinkled bag of M&Ms resting in his lap. Abe. Her grandfather. He rose carefully as she approached, leaning on his cane, as surprised to see her as she was to see him.

"Grandpa?" Her voice trembled, caught between relief and confusion. "Did you come to get me?"

His lined face softened, though his eyes were troubled. "What are you doing here, honey? Are you in trouble?"

She shook her head quickly. "No. We just… we went out to the woods. Tried to get some video of the monster."

The way she said it—half guilty, half defiant— made him frown. "You're okay?"

"Just tired. Hungry."

He offered her the bag of candy without a word. She took a few pieces, let the chocolate dissolve on her tongue, then slid the rest into her coat pocket. "Why are you here?"

"I came to talk to someone."

"Talk to who? Why?" Her voice softened with worry.

Abe's gaze drifted down the hallway toward the closed interview rooms. "I saw a video. That thing in the woods..." His jaw tightened. "I think I know what's going on. Or at least... who."

Her stomach dropped. "Who?"

For a moment, his eyes clouded with something

like shame. Then, barely above a whisper: "Priscilla's boy. Matthew."

Her eyes lit up. "Grandpa, I know it's him…"

Footsteps and the sounds of a man clearing his throat drew their attention. Chief Hodges came striding down the corridor, papers in hand. His brow was set in its usual furrow until his eyes found the old man waiting with a young lady at his side. Something about the man gave him pause. He slowed, his gaze narrowing as he studied him.

"Good evening, sir," Hodges said carefully. "Have we met?"

Abe lifted an eyebrow, his voice low and steady. "You were there…"

Shelley's eyes darted to her grandfather, puzzled by the exchange. Hodges gave a small shake of his head, as though to clear it, then said, "They told me you wanted to speak with me."

Abe nodded once. He cast a glance toward Shelley before answering. "I think I can help."

The chief regarded him curiously, then motioned down the hall. "Right this way, sir."

"Please," Abe replied, "call me Abe."

Before following, he bent to Shelley, his voice soft but firm. "You head on home, sweetheart." He pressed a kiss to her forehead. She stayed rooted where she was, watching as her grandfather's tall frame disappeared beside the chief into the shadows of the hall. The office door shut behind them, leaving her standing alone.

Inside, the air smelled of burnt coffee and old paper. Hodges sank into his chair, eyes fixed on the abnormally tall man across from him. The silence stretched until it became almost unbearable. Abe set his cane against his knee and lowered himself into the opposite chair, his hands folding over one another.

"You helped me out of the creek that night," Abe said at last.

Hodges exhaled sharply, the memory flickering across his face. He gave a short nod. "Yes, sir. I believe I did. First week on the force, as a matter of fact. Worked thirty-six hours straight. Chased a damn tiger… Went home and told my wife if every week was like that, I'd see if my uncle could get me on at the Ford plant."

A chuckle, quiet and rough, escaped Abe. Hodges leaned back, shaking his head as the memory settled heavier between them.

"They called off the search for that little boy a few days later," Hodges went on, his voice quieting, "but some of us kept looking another week or two. Disappeared without a trace."

Abe leaned forward, his tone carrying the gravity of someone who had come to end a silence long kept. "Well, that's why I'm here."

The chief's brow furrowed. "They said you had information about whatever's out there in the woods."

"Yes, sir," Abe said evenly. "That little boy's name was Matthew Jones." He let the words hang a moment, heavy in the dim light. "What if he's still out there?"

Hodges stilled, his eyes locked on the old man. Whatever fatigue had dulled his face was gone now. Abe had his full attention.

Contact

Morning broke gray and uncertain, mist coiling low between the trees. The trestle loomed in the distance, a black silhouette carved against the pale sky. At the edge of the woods, a row of black SWAT vans idled, their engines rumbling like caged animals. Harsh floodlights cut into the fog, beams stretching into the forest's teeth.

Chief Hodges stood with Captain Dunn, the SWAT commander, whose broad chest strained against his tactical vest. Behind them, twelve armed men spread into formation, silent and grim.

"You're sure you're ready for this?" Hodges asked quietly.

Dunn's face was stone. "If it bleeds, we can take it down. But the goal is capture."

Hodges nodded, though the word *capture* tasted foolish in the air.

The squad disappeared into the trees, boots muffled by damp leaves. The deeper they pressed, the more the woods resisted. Sound itself seemed to shrink. No birds. No insects. Only the rasp of their own gear, the drag of breath behind black visors.

Then, a sound. A bleat, thin and stretched, carried strangely on the wind. Too warped to be animal.

At the rear of the formation, Officer Whitaker froze. He swore he heard a rustle in the brush. "Captain..." His voice trembled.

Dunn raised a fist. The line stopped dead, weapons aimed, listening. Silence fell thick.

Whitaker scanned the shadows. Just undergrowth shifting with the fog. He gave the all-clear and turned back—

Something black erupted from the brush. An arm, impossibly long, hooked around his throat and yanked him into the dark before he could make a sound. His bones cracked like a green branch, the noise carrying in the stillness. Then nothing.

The line spun, weapons raised, hearts pounding. Whitaker was gone.

They pushed into a clearing, sweat and fear crawling their necks.

"Movement," one officer hissed, pointing into a wall of brush.

Dunn's reply came low and steady through the radio. "Close in slow."

The team circled. One officer yanked a flashbang from his vest. "Flash out."

He tossed it. A second of silence, then—
POP–CRACK!

White light tore the clearing open, followed by a thunderclap that shook the trees. The earth seemed to lurch. From the smoke, shapes burst forth— a dozen goats, wild-eyed and frantic, scattering in a blind stampede.

And then came the thing.

It rose from the heart of the smoke, hulking and half-human, swaying under the aftershock. Mud-caked hair clung to its massive frame, dripping in thick ropes. Its eyes, dark as oil, flickered in the light. It grabbed at its ears, a guttural cry breaking from its chest— a sound both mournful and monstrous.

The officers hesitated, riveted in place. One whispered, "What the hell is that?"

Dunn's command cut through the paralysis.

"Taser! Now!"

The shot cracked. Prongs buried in its chest. Electricity surged, making the creature convulse, every muscle seizing before it dropped hard to its knees.

The team swarmed, boots pounding the ground.

"It's human," one said, disbelief thick in his voice.

"No," another spat, "too much hair. Too much…"

The creature groaned, dazed, but breathing. Then it lifted its head, and for the briefest moment its eyes were clear. Human. Haunted. Pleading.

The men faltered. Guns stayed raised but fingers hovered uncertain over triggers.

"Cuff it!" someone barked.

Two edged forward, one with reinforced shackles, the other covering him. The cuffs snapped over wrists and ankles, the body slumping with a low, broken bleat.

From behind them came Hodges' voice, cold and resolute. "Get it on the gurney. Sedate it. Contain it. Now."

The squad moved quickly, heaving the restrained creature onto a reinforced gurney, its guttural breaths rasping through the straps and muzzle. Floodlights cut pale slices through the mist, guiding them back toward the vans.

Then—movement.

A shout went up from the line. One of the officers had spotted a shape dragging itself through the wet leaves.

"Contact, left side!"

Flashlights cut across the ground, beams locking onto a figure crawling toward them. Whitaker. His face was ashen, one arm twisted grotesquely against his chest, blood soaking the collar of his uniform. His lips moved soundlessly as he tried to speak, his body jerking with each shallow pull forward.

"Jesus…" one officer breathed, rushing to him. "He's alive."

Whitaker's eyes rolled back as they lifted him, his broken body trembling. He tried to lift a hand — pointing weakly toward the trees. His mouth formed the same word again and again, barely a whisper:

"Run!"

♦ ♦ ♦ ♦ ♦ ♦

Rows of fluorescent lights hummed faintly overhead as Mr. Stringer paced at the front of the classroom, chalk dust streaked across his elbow. He spoke with the animated cadence of a man trying to make history sound alive.

"Andrew Jackson was an attorney, a judge, and eventually a commander of the army," Stringer said, tapping the chalk against the board. "He even killed a man in a duel. But he's best known, of course, as our seventh president."

A voice from the middle row piped up. "Wait… did he really shoot somebody?"

Stringer half-smiled, enjoying the spark of curiosity. "He did. Charles Dickinson, in 1806. Jackson took a bullet to the chest, but he stayed standing long enough to raise his pistol and fire back. Dickinson died. And Jackson carried that ball in his chest the rest of his life."

A low murmur passed through the students. Some leaned in with fascination, others smirked at the idea of a president actually pulling a trigger.

At the window, Jimmy barely looked up. His pen dragged across the page, not notes but sketches — shadows and shapes more than words. The duel, his brother's face, the trestle looming in the background. A tangle of his thoughts spilled in ink.

Then he felt it.

A tremor in the air. Buzzing. Vibrations.

Around him, phones lit up one after another. Students leaned down, checking their screens, whispers blooming across the room like sparks.

"Okay," Stringer said, half-joking, trying to rein them in. "Either the Cardinals won the National Championship or Russia dropped a bomb on New York City. What's going on?"

From the back, a boy with glasses blurted it out before anyone else could.

"They caught it! That creature out in the woods — they caught it!"

Gasps. Murmurs. The class erupted in a tide of noise.

Jimmy's head snapped up, heart slamming in his chest. His phone buzzed against his desk, the vibration crawling into his bones. With a quick, practiced motion, he unlocked it. The glow of the screen washed across his face.

LIVE – WLKL-13 NEWS SPECIAL REPORT.

His pulse quickened. The voices of his classmates faded into nothing. All that mattered was the headline. All that mattered was the screen. The monster that killed his brother and uncle had finally been caught.

A grim smile tugged at the corner of his mouth.

The bell rang, jarring, and Jimmy was already on his feet, shoving books into his bag. He needed to find

Shelley. He needed to see what happened next.

The hallway exploded with bodies, lockers clanging, phones raised. Screens glowed in every hand. Jimmy wove through the crush, scanning faces until... there.

Shelley rounded the corner. Their eyes locked.

"You see the news?" he asked, breathless.

She nodded once. "You?"

"Yeah."

They slipped into the shallow nook by the vending machines, phones raised in sync, tuned to the same feed.

Onscreen, Chief Hodges stood at a podium before a curtain of blue. Reporters shouted over one another, voices tinny through the speaker. Hodges gripped the sides of the podium, his face drawn, his uniform hat tilted low over tired eyes.

"There was an incident this morning in the woods near Pope Lick Creek," he said into the microphone. "I can't say much right now. The investigation is... well, it's complicated."

He adjusted his hat, looked away, then back to the cameras.

"But I can tell you this... we believe the community is safe. Everyone can sleep a little bit better tonight."

His gaze flicked off camera. "There will be a formal press conference later this week, once more details are confirmed. I want to thank the Louisville Police Department and the SWAT team for their swift action."

A pause. He leaned closer, voice firm. "The nightmare is over."

And with that, he stepped back. The feed filled with shouted questions he ignored.

Shelley lowered her phone slowly, her lips parting. Her voice was soft, uncertain.

"The nightmare is over?"

Jimmy didn't answer. He only looked at her, searching her face, his own doubts a mirror of hers. Neither believed it. Not really.

◆ ◆ ◆ ◆ ◆ ◆

Later that evening, a reinforced steel door clanked open at the end of the detention wing. Chief Hodges walked ahead, leading Abe through a corridor that gleamed like glass beneath the humming overhead lights. Armed guards stood every few feet like statues, rifles angled but ready. Abe, dressed now in a clean button-up shirt, looked almost out of place in the sterile procession.

"You don't have to do this," Hodges muttered, his tone somewhere between warning and plea. "We've got experts inbound. Doctors. Biologists. The sharpest guys over at U of L."

Abe's long stride never slowed. "No doctor can explain what I think I already know."

Hodges shot him a sidelong glance. "Do you really think he'll remember you?"

Abe's shoulders lifted in a weary shrug.

They stopped at a heavy, electronically locked door. Two guards stepped forward, swiping keycards in tandem. Metal locks groaned, then released with a mechanical thunk. Hodges squared himself, his hand brushing against his holster.

"Don't get too close," he warned.

The door swung inward.

The containment room was low-lit and humid, air

thick like a greenhouse left untended. In the center loomed a steel holding cell. Inside, the creature paced on all fours like a restless predator, its orange jumpsuit hanging awkwardly over a body too animal for human clothes. Its hairy feet bulged against shoes not made to contain them. When its eyes caught Abe's frame, it bared its crooked, yellowed teeth.

The room vibrated with tension.

Abe stepped forward. At first the creature snarled, but then it stopped. Its head tilted. The low rumble that left its chest carried a note less of menace than of puzzlement.

"Matthew?" Abe's voice was low, fragile.

The name seemed to strike something. The creature blinked, flinched almost imperceptibly, its pacing slowing.

"Son... do you remember me?" Abe's voice cracked on the words.

The thing sniffed the air, brow furrowing. Abe dared another step closer. Hodges' hand slid toward his weapon.

"Abe," Hodges hissed. "Please. Don't."

"Just a second," Abe said, eyes never leaving the creature.

He raised his hand — open, trembling — and extended it toward the bars.

The creature lunged.

CLANG! Its massive fingers locked around Abe's hand through the steel. Hodges whipped his gun free, heart pounding.

"Back! Back up now!"

"NO!" Abe's voice was stern, commanding. "Don't shoot!"

The grip was strong, too strong, but it wasn't crushing him. The creature pressed Abe's hand to its face, inhaling deeply.

"You remember," Abe whispered. "Don't you?"

For a long, harrowing beat, the room seemed to hold its breath. The creature's ragged breathing slowed. At last, it released Abe's hand. Slowly, almost delicately, it retreated to the cot in the corner, curling up tight—knees to chest, arms wrapped around itself. Its eyes closed. It looked, impossibly, like a frightened child.

Hodges lowered his gun, words catching in his throat. "I don't believe it..."

"I do," Abe murmured. His eyes never left the figure. "It is him. I was there the night he disappeared."

Silence stretched, broken only by the creature's unsteady breaths. Hodges found his voice again. "Are his parents still alive?"

Abe nodded faintly. "Last I heard. I got a Christmas card from them last year. They're in Alabama... on the coast. Orange Beach, I think."

Hodges holstered his weapon. "We need them here. As soon as possible."

◆ ◆ ◆ ◆ ◆ ◆

The front door opened and closed with a quiet click that seemed too soft for a man of Chief Hodges' size. He was tired, the kind of bone-deep weariness that came after a day of chasing an urban legend. The warm smell of roast beef and carrots filled the air. His wife, Kathy appeared from the living room, wiping her hands on a dish towel.

"Supper's on the stove if you're hungry," she said

softly. "Mashed potatoes are in the fridge."

"Thanks, honey," he sighed, loosening his tie. "Long day. There are some things I need to look into before I go to bed."

She glanced at the clock on the wall. "Wendell, it's nine-thirty."

"I'm sorry," he said, rubbing his temples. "This Goatman thing is pressing on me. The governor's office called today wanting updates. Lots of eyes on this. Got people in Alabama involved now. I just need to look at some stuff and I'll try to wind down."

Kathy gave him a look—the one that mixed concern with resignation. She had been married to the chief of police for a long time; she knew how some cases burrowed under his skin. He gave her a kiss on the cheek.

"Well," she said, "I'm going to read my Bible and then head to bed."

"Love you," he said.

She gave a faint smile and turned for the hallway. "You looked very handsome on the news today." He let out a small snicker and shook his head as she walked away.

Hodges moved into the den and sank into his old recliner, clicking on the television. It was already on the local news, and Trey Robertson's polished face filled the screen. "...and while Chief Hodges assured the public 'the nightmare is over,' many are still wondering what exactly that meant. Hopefully, there will be more answers in the morning." Hodges grunted and turned it off with a sharp click. He stood up, the silence of the room preferable to the noise.

He moved to his desk and opened his laptop. An

email from the Alabama Highway Patrol was waiting, asking for clarity on what the Louisville Police Department needed. He typed a quick reply, stating his office would call in the morning with specifics. He sent the email and leaned back, staring blankly at the computer screen. Now, there was nothing to do but wait.

He found himself drawn to the hall closet, pulling down a dusty cardboard box from the top shelf. He brought it into the kitchen. The year 1978 was scrawled on the side in faded marker. Inside, beneath old commendations and yellowed newspaper clippings, was a thin manila folder. TRAIN WRECK – POPE LICK – OCT. '78.

His fingers, thicker now with age, trembled slightly as he opened it. He bypassed the gruesome photos of the crash until he found a small, stapled report he had written himself. His own handwriting, so much neater then, detailed the scene. Tucked inside was a small, grainy Polaroid of a large suitcase lying half-buried in the mud. On the back, he had written a note:

Matthew Jones, Age 3, MISSING.

Hodges stared at the words. Over a forty-year career filled with murders, robberies, and every kind of human ugliness, it was this case—not a crime, but a disappearance—that had settled deepest in his bones. It was the ghost that never left. The little boy swallowed by the woods.

He had always imagined the boy's fate, a sad, quick end in the dark. He had never imagined this. The ghost hadn't just returned; it had become the monster from the town's oldest urban legend. A quiet promise he'd made to himself as a young cop—to find out what happened to that boy now felt like a debt come due. He closed the folder, the weight of it feeling heavier than it had any right to be.

"Momma's Here"

The next morning, the sun beat down on a dusty gravel road winding through a tired Alabama trailer park. Rusting awnings sagged above dented mailboxes. A chorus of tinkling wind chimes competed with the distant whine of cicadas. In one yard, a flock of sun-bleached plastic flamingos clustered together, their cracked necks and faded pink bodies standing sentinel before a silver trailer whose roof was the color of rust.

A marked Alabama State Patrol cruiser rolled up, tires crunching in the gravel. Dust plumed in its wake as two troopers stepped out. Davis, mid-forties, carried himself with the weary professionalism of a man who'd seen it all. Reynolds, younger, shifted awkwardly at his side, already sweating through his collar.

"This the one?" Davis asked.

"Unit six," Reynolds confirmed, pointing. "Flamingos and all."

Davis squinted at the cracked plastic flock and muttered, "Classy." Then he rapped firmly on the door.

There was a pause, then the door swung open.

Priscilla stood in the frame. Age had whittled her down but hadn't dulled her presence. Seventies now, pale, wide-eyed, wrapped in a faded pink bathrobe. A scarf bound back her gray hair, but what caught Reynolds off guard was the beard—full, graying, neatly combed. Her tattooed eyebrows, sharp and arched, lent her an almost theatrical expression.

The moment she saw their uniforms, she slammed the door shut.

Reynolds blinked, leaned in. "Did she have a…"

"Yep," Davis cut him off without missing a beat.

Silence hung heavy until the door creaked back open. Priscilla reappeared, breathing hard, one hand pressed to her chest.

Behind her emerged Willie. Seventies as well, deeply tanned, skin leathered by time and sun. He was shirtless, wearing nothing but a leopard-print speedo that clung to his stout frame. He blinked into the daylight like it was a stage light.

"Officers," Priscilla rasped, her voice trembling. "I can assure you my husband was acting in self-defense. That man in the produce aisle was asking for it. He said some of the meanest, most awful things…"

Reynolds coughed into his fist. "Uh, ma'am… we're not here about that."

Davis stepped in, steady. "We've been sent to escort you both to the airport."

Priscilla tilted her head, eyes narrowing like a hawk.

Davis continued, carefully. "We have reason to believe… your son, Matthew, may still be alive."

Her face cracked. "If this is a joke," she said, voice breaking, "it's not funny."

She pressed herself against the doorframe, trembling.

Willie stepped forward, his anger flaring hot. "What did you say?" He jabbed Davis in the stomach with a bony finger. "This is not something to joke about. Who put you up to this? Was it Sterling? That bastard. I knew it was Sterling…" He muttered, pacing in a small circle, fury unraveling into disbelief.

Priscilla collapsed into sobs, covering her mouth with both hands. The troopers exchanged a quick glance, struggling to remain stone-faced.

"Look, ma'am," Davis said firmly. "We're not here for pranks. This came from our sergeant, working with Louisville PD. They think they have your boy. There's a plane waiting. But we need to leave. Now."

Priscilla's sobs turned into sharp gasps. "Oh my God... Matthew?" She turned and scurried inside, robe trailing behind her like a cape.

Willie lingered. The tough façade drained away, leaving a man trembling at the edges. His voice dropped low, raw. "Is he... really alive?"

Davis held his gaze. "I don't have all the answers, sir. Just orders to get you to Louisville."

Willie stood there for a long moment, blinking as though trying to wake from a dream. Then, slowly, he nodded. "I'll be right back."

The former little strongman shuffled inside, closing the door behind him with a long, tired creak.

Inside, the trailer, Priscilla scrambled from room to room, dragging dresses and scarves from hangers, stuffing them into a faded suitcase that wouldn't shut no matter how she pressed her weight on it. Willie moved slower, methodical, tossing clothes and bottles of lotion and shampoo into his own case.

Priscilla gave the stubborn case one last slam of her palm before letting out a frustrated groan. "It won't close!"

Willie glanced at her, then sighed. Without a word, he pushed open the door and stepped outside into the daylight.

Trooper Davis shifted at the bottom of the steps. "You ready?"

Willie shook his head quickly. "Uh... not yet."

He scurried across the gravel to the crooked little shed behind the trailer. Rusted hinges screamed as he yanked it open. A moment later he emerged with a bundle of cracked rubber straps in hand, grinning with a strange, boyish pride.

"Be right back," he said, moving past the troopers with a spring in his step.

Inside again, he knelt down beside Priscilla's case and cinched the straps tight, crisscrossing them until the bulging suitcase finally held its shape.

Priscilla wiped at her eyes, voice breaking as she whispered, "Thank you, honey..."

Willie winked at her, trying to muster strength neither of them had. "Come on," he said, tugging the case upright. "We gotta go."

Priscilla clutched his arm as they pulled the suitcases toward the door, both moving like people in a dream, fear and hope weighing heavier than anything they'd packed.

They emerged from the trailer together, lugging the two suitcases down the wobbling steps. Reynolds spotted the rubber straps crisscrossing Priscilla's case and slowed. Willie caught the look and smirked.

"Couldn't find the duct tape," he said.

Reynolds raised his brows at Davis, who fought back a chuckle and failed.

Reynolds straightened, trying to recover his authority. "Please, Mr. and Mrs. Jones," he said, gesturing toward the cruiser. "Right this way."

Just as they started forward, Priscilla stopped dead and turned back toward the trailer, a look of panic on her face. Willie and the officers gave a confused look.

"I think I left my curling iron plugged in!" she

shouted over her shoulder.

Willie shook his head, his irritation showing. "Damnit, Pris! Let's get going!"

She rushed back inside. Willie turned to the troopers. "Sorry, boys," he muttered. A moment later, she burst back out the door. "Okay, we're good to go."

As they settled into the back of the cruiser, Willie leaned over to her. "Was it plugged in?"

She didn't respond at first, just stared straight ahead. He glared at her until she finally sighed.

"No," she admitted quietly. "It's in my suitcase."

Willie stared at her for a long second, and then couldn't help but let out a low chuckle, shaking his head.

◆ ◆ ◆ ◆ ◆ ◆

Four hours later, a small charter jet rolled to a stop beneath the glare of floodlights. Inside the private terminal, Hodges stood rigid, clipboard in hand, while Abe lingered a few paces back, arms folded across his chest. His jacket was pressed, his face taut with a mixture of dread and longing.

Willie nudged Priscilla. She only groaned, head lolling against the seatback, scarf slipping down her shoulder.

"Come on, woman," Willie barked, louder this time.

Priscilla snorted herself half-awake, blinking slowly, confused. She rubbed at her eyes, still drifting somewhere between sleep and disbelief. Finally, with a sharp inhale, she jolted upright.

Her oversized sunglasses sat crooked on her nose. She shuffled to her feet in mismatched travel clothes—

patterned leggings, an enormous coat that nearly swallowed her frame — and though her eyes were puffy and wet, her beard was neatly combed, as if even exhaustion hadn't stripped her of pride. A balled tissue trembled in her fist.

Willie followed, dressed down in sweatpants and a bowling shirt.

The moment Abe saw her, his face broke. His breath hitched in his throat.

"Priscilla…"

She froze. For a beat, time suspended itself in the sterile light of the hangar.

"Abe?" Her voice cracked, trembling.

Then she was moving, rushing across the floor, tears spilling. "Is it true?"

Abe nodded, voice low. "I saw him."

Priscilla clutched her mouth, gasping through her sobs. Willie, still trying to keep his shoulders square, faltered when Abe turned and kneeled in front of him. The two men embraced.

"I missed you, big guy…" Willie muttered thickly into his old friend's shoulder.

Hodges stepped forward at last, breaking the spell. "Mr. and Mrs. Jones, I'm Chief Hodges," he said gently. A beat passed, his eyes flicking between their guarded faces. "You probably don't remember, but I was there the night your son disappeared."

Priscilla and Willie exchanged blank, uneasy stares. Neither spoke.

Hodges cleared his throat, his tone shifting to something almost paternal. "We've got a secure facility ten minutes from here. I'll take you to him personally."

Willie's eyes narrowed, suspicion bristling in his

voice. "What kind of secure facility?"

"One where no one can hurt him. Or panic," Hodges said carefully. "He's not exactly what you remember. But he's alive. And he reacted to Abe. That's why we called you."

Priscilla and Willie exchanged a look — hers trembling with hope, his stiff with guarded fear.

"You hear that, Pris?" Willie's hand pressed to his chest. "We're gonna see our boy." His voice cracked despite himself. "He in some kind of trouble?"

Priscilla dabbed at her eyes with the crumpled tissue, chin lifting, resolve written in the tight line of her mouth.

Hodges gave a measured nod. "There's a lot we need to talk about. Please… follow me."

He led them from the terminal into the cool night air, where two black sedans idled at the curb. He gestured for Abe, Willie, and Priscilla to get in the first one. "We'll go over everything when we get to the facility," he said, before climbing into the second car with another officer to follow them.

Inside the car, Priscilla couldn't stop fidgeting, her hands twisting the damp tissue in her lap. "Is he okay?" she asked the officer driving, her voice a frantic whisper. "How are they treating him? Where is he being held? Is he scared?"

Abe, sitting beside her, placed a large, gentle hand on her arm. "He's safe, Priscilla." He paused, his voice low. "I saw him. I think… I think he remembered me."

Willie, in the front passenger seat, turned around, his face a mask of disbelief. "Are you sure, Abe? After all this time?"

"I'm sure," Abe said, his gaze unwavering. "It's

him."

Priscilla wiped away a fresh wave of tears, and they sat in silence for a long time as the car sped through the darkened city streets. Finally, Willie broke the quiet.

"You ever hear from Stetson?" he asked, his eyes finding Abe's in the rearview mirror. "Or anyone from the show?"

Abe shook his head slowly. "Not really. Just you two, now and then. Margie used to write me after the accident."

Willie smirked, a flash of his old self. "What about Ally?"

Priscilla reached up and punched him in the arm. Abe's expression grew quiet, distant. "Last I heard, she and her sister were living in an assisted living home out in California."

Willie looked out the window, his smirk fading. "I always thought you two would wind up together," he said softly.

Abe just sighed, the memory of his old flame weighing on him. He quickly changed the subject.

"Margie tried to go back to the show, you know," he added, his voice heavy. "After her arm healed up. But she got real sick not long after. Moved back home to New York where she grew up. She would send me letters sometimes. But I… I haven't heard from her in a long time. I imagine she…" His voice trailed off, the unspoken words hanging in the car's quiet interior.

Willie nodded slowly, his gaze distant. "Margie was a sweet gal. Sure do miss her."

"I heard Rusty got his arm ripped off by a lion, working for a circus down in Tampa," Priscilla chimed in, her voice flat. Abe winced at the thought. "Someone also told me Stetson was selling used cars in Tallahassee."

Willie chuckled, a dry, rattling sound. "Sounds about right."

"What about you two?" Abe asked, his voice gentle. "How did you end up in Alabama?"

Priscilla looked down at her hands. "We tried to keep going," she said, her painted lips a tight line. "Stetson said the show must go on, but my heart wasn't in it. After we lost Matty... the people looked different. Meaner. The whispers felt louder. One day, I just couldn't take it anymore." She took a steadying breath. "So I quit. Went to cosmetology school, of all things. Shaved off the beard and decided if I was going to be stared at, I might as well be by the beach."

"She's a hell of a hairdresser," Willie added from the front seat. "I took a job as a maintenance man at the local elementary. It wasn't too bad. The kids were a lot of fun. Fixed leaky faucets, unclogged toilets, patched up walls. Honest work."

"We just wanted quiet," Priscilla finished, her voice barely a whisper.

The car slowed, turning into a gated, high-security complex. The officer driving glanced to the elderly sideshow attractions in the back. "We're here."

Priscilla tensed immediately, her hands gripping her purse. Willie reached back and put a steadying hand on her leg. Abe offered a soft, reassuring smile.

"Priscilla," he said gently. "Breathe."

Chief Hodges led them down a sterile corridor, his steady stride echoing off concrete walls. Fluorescent panels buzzed above, casting pale light over the polished floor. Willie and Priscilla followed close behind, their eyes darting nervously to the guards stationed at intervals along the hall. Priscilla clutched a balled tissue in one hand, the other twitching at her side, while Willie silently worried that this was all somehow tied to the incident in the produce aisle at the grocery store a month earlier.

Abe walked between them, tall and unshaken, though the lines of guilt on his face were etched deep. He noticed the tremor in Priscilla's hands and laid a broad, reassuring palm on her shoulder. "It'll be alright," he murmured. She gave the smallest nod but didn't meet his eyes.

At the end of the corridor, Hodges paused at a heavy door. He glanced back at the three of them, his expression serious. "Please," he said, pushing it open. "Come on in."

They stepped into a square visitation room, barren save for a metal table and four hard-backed chairs. The air was close, carrying a faint tang of disinfectant. Hodges gestured for them to sit, then remained standing.

The air in the visitation room was thick, the silence hanging heavier than the smell itself. A manila folder lay like a stone between them on the table, Hodges' hand resting on it as though it might spring open on its own.

"Your son is being charged with five counts of murder," he said flatly. "Two of which were police officers."

The words hit like a hammer. Priscilla's hand flew to her chest, her eyes filling before the sound of her gasp had even faded. "My baby couldn't kill anyone. He wouldn't..."

Hodges' expression softened, but his voice did not. "Ma'am, I don't know what happened to him out there. No one does. But the charges are serious. Kentucky still has the death penalty." He paused, the weight of it settling over the table. "Hasn't been used in years, but... this could change that."

Willie shifted, the swagger gone from his shoulders. His tan skin seemed drained of every drop of color. Abe kept still, shoulders rigid, but his silence was heavy with knowledge.

"Now," Hodges went on, "because of his condition—whatever you want to call it—the courts may lean toward life in a facility." He lifted his eyes, meeting theirs one by one. "But I can't promise anything. This case is... unprecedented."

The word lingered. Priscilla clutched at her tissue, nodding through tears. Willie gave only the barest of nods, reluctant, as though agreeing to face something he'd avoided for decades. Abe's steady presence was the only anchor at the table.

"You ready to see him?" Hodges asked.

Priscilla's answer came before the question was finished—an eager, broken nod. Willie hesitated, then sighed and gave his reluctant assent.

The walk down the corridor felt endless. Two armed guards scanned their keycards at the secure door, the electronic lock buzzing open with a hollow click. The walls seemed to close in, sterile and humming faintly with unseen machines.

"What you're about to see might be hard to process," Hodges warned, his hand lingering on the handle.

Priscilla pressed forward without hesitation, trembling but determined. Willie lagged behind, his steps faltering. Abe bent down, steadying him with a hand on his shoulder, before guiding both of them inside.

The cell block was dim and echoing, lined with iron and shadows. In the center, behind reinforced bars, lay the creature—massive and hunched, its frame swamped by an orange jumpsuit that fit more like a costume than clothing. Bare feet sprawled over the edge of the cot, nails long and curled.

At the sound of the door, it stirred. A low groan, a rustle of fabric, and then it rose—slowly, warily—until its full size seemed to press against the air itself.

Priscilla's eyes widened. Her hand flew to her mouth. "My baby," she whispered, her voice breaking.

Willie froze, his mouth open, words failing him. Priscilla took a faltering step closer, tears welling. "Momma's here," she said softly.

The creature stepped forward, cautious, its head low. It stopped at the bars, studying the faces gathered before it. Its eyes moved from Abe to Hodges, then stopped—locked on Priscilla.

Something flickered.

Recognition.

Willie stumbled backward. His eyes dropped to the floor as if afraid to look at what stood before him. Abe steadied him again, but Willie's voice came out broken. "Oh no..."

"Do you recognize these people?" Hodges asked quietly.

The creature tilted its head, eyes fixed on Priscilla. It opened its mouth. At first, only a strangled bleat emerged, a pitiful sound somewhere between animal and man. Then, with painful effort…

"Ma…"

Another attempt.

"Momma…"

The word tore through the silence like a blade. Everyone gasped.

Priscilla rushed forward until her fingers nearly brushed the bars. The creature recoiled at first, like a spooked animal, but then inched closer. Sniffing, testing. Slowly, trembling, it lowered its enormous head until it rested against her outstretched palm.

"Oh, my baby," she sobbed, stroking coarse hair as tears streamed down her face.

The sound of her weeping changed him. The creature's expression twisted, not with rage, but with something deeper, more bewildered. He tilted his head, studying her as though he couldn't comprehend the sound of grief, as though her pain was an unsolvable riddle.

Abe turned away, overcome, tears falling. Willie slumped to the floor, his hands cradling his head.

The door banged open behind them.

"Chief," Officer Cole said, his voice grim. "We found this near the bodies of Stark and Morales."

All eyes turned. Cole stepped inside, holding up a clear evidence bag.

Inside was a tattered, water-stained Raggedy Andy doll.

The creature froze. Its pupils dilated, nostrils flaring. A thin, shuddering inhale filled the room. A memory seemed to pass across its face, unspoken but undeniable — a flicker of laughter, a shadow of something lost.

Then it erupted.

The cell shook as the creature hurled itself at the bars, screaming with a sound that was more pain than fury. Steel rang under the assault.

"Matthew!" Priscilla shrieked, stumbling backward.

Cole recoiled. Hodges snapped orders. "Put it away! Now!"

Cole fumbled, shoving the doll back into the bag, hiding it behind his back. But the damage was done. The creature clawed at the bars, reaching, sobbing, its voice raw with something primal and broken.

"Everybody out! Now!" Hodges barked.

Abe wrapped an arm around Priscilla, dragging her toward the door. Willie staggered after them. Guards swarmed in as Hodges lingered for one last glance.

The creature had collapsed to its knees, clutching the bars, wailing like a child in the dark.

"God help us..." Hodges whispered, shaken, before turning away.

The door slammed shut behind them.

In the hallway, Priscilla buried her face against Abe's chest, her body wracked with sobs. Abe managed to hold his composure, holding her close. Willie leaned against the wall, trembling, overwhelmed.

Her cries were suddenly cut short by a sound from behind the steel door. It was a muted, strange, and deeply sad goatlike bleat. Priscilla stopped crying, her head lifting from Abe's chest. She, Abe, and Willie all turned their eyes to Hodges. The chief looked from their haunted faces back toward the door. The hallway fell silent for a beat.

Then it came again, louder this time — a racking, soblike bleat that echoed with an agony beyond human words.

"What was that?" Willie whispered, his voice hoarse.

Hodges just shook his head, his own expression grim. "Come on," he said softly. "We need to go."

As he began to usher them away, Priscilla lost it again, pulling against Abe's arm. "Is he okay?" she cried. "Is my baby okay?"

Abe glanced back at the steel door before turning away.

"Please," Hodges said, his voice heavy. "Come with me." He gently guided them down the hall, leaving only the echo of that terrible, lonely sound behind them.

Goatman Fever

The next morning, the press room at City Hall was packed, every seat filled, cameras perched on tripods, microphones bristling from the podium. A low murmur buzzed across the room until Chief Hodges appeared, broad-shouldered and grim, flanked by two men — Dr. Michael Rumsey of the University of Louisville and District Attorney Lester Lee.

Hodges stepped to the microphone, his expression carved from stone. "There's been a lot of speculation, rumors, and — frankly — misinformation about what's going on in the Pope Lick area," he began, pausing until the shuffle of notebooks and the clicking of pens settled. "I hope to bring a little more clarity today."

He leaned forward, voice hardening. "Yes, there has been an arrest in the recent murders." His fist struck the podium with a heavy thud. "And I want to be absolutely clear: there is no monster. The suspect is forty-three-year-old Matthew Jones."

The name hung in the air like smoke. Hodges gave a curt nod and stepped to the side, motioning to Dr. Rumsey.

Rumsey moved to the podium with the cautious air of a man carrying something fragile. His glasses slid low on his nose as he peered at the crowd. "Ladies and gentlemen... in over thirty-five years of medical practice and research, I have never seen anything like this."

He steadied himself, choosing his words. "Since his detainment, my colleagues and I have observed and treated Mr. Jones. He suffers from a rare genetic condition known as hypertrichosis — commonly referred to as 'werewolf syndrome.'"

The words triggered a collective gasp, a ripple of disbelief cutting through the room. Rumsey shook his head, silencing them. "It is, without question, the most extreme case I have ever encountered. Mr. Jones is covered in dense, dark hair from head to toe. He exhibits neurological trauma, primitive survival traits. His muscle development is extraordinary, but so are his cognitive deficits."

He raised his notes but hardly glanced at them. "Chronologically, he is a man in his forties. But emotionally? Mentally? He is the boy who disappeared four decades ago. His prolonged isolation has stunted him. He lacks the capacity for complex reasoning or language. There's no telling what horrors he endured in those woods. When I examined him, I removed three ticks from his back."

The room was silent, hanging on his every word.

"He is, quite literally, a man raised in the wild — by goats, I believe. To survive, he adapted. He became an apex predator, not through strategy, but through animal cunning. His behavior resembles that of the herd… skittish, territorial, aggressive when threatened."

Rumsey's tone softened, his shoulders sinking. "This man… this boy… has lived through a tragedy none of us can comprehend. I urge you all to hold both compassion and restraint in your hearts. Pray for him. He has lived through hell."

He stepped back, the weight of his words still hanging when Lester Lee, the District Attorney, approached.

"This is," Lee began smoothly, his voice edged with the polish of politics, "an extraordinarily complex case. We are seeking a full mental health evaluation, though Mr. Jones' condition makes that difficult." His eyes swept across the crowd, settling briefly on Rumsey before hardening again. "That said, we must not forget the victims—Johnny Summers, Cynthia Murphy, Arnold Summers, and Officers Michael Stark and Diego Morales. Their lives were taken. And justice will be served."

He stepped aside.

The press erupted—voices clashing, questions shouted over one another. *Dr. Rumsey, do you believe… Did he know what he was doing?*

Chief Hodges returned to the microphone, jaw tight. "No questions. I'm sorry." He motioned to his officers, who moved to shut the event down.

Flashes strobed. Reporters scrambled, their voices colliding in a storm of frustration as the officials filed out, leaving only the echo of unanswered questions behind.

◆ ◆ ◆ ◆ ◆ ◆

Jimmy kept his head down as he cut across Main Street, hands shoved deep in his jacket pockets. The autumn air had cooled sharp, the kind of chill that carried the smell of fried grease and damp leaves all at once. He didn't want to be here, didn't want to see the window displays that had turned his brother's death into a punchline.

But there they were.

A chalkboard outside Megan's Market advertised "Try our NEW Goatman Chili! It's no so baaaaaad." in sloppy white letters. Across the street, the local screen-printing shop had filled its front window with racks of T-shirts. Black cotton, a snarling goat's head beneath the trestle silhouette, and in bold letters: "GOATMAN MADE ME DO IT." He caught his own reflection superimposed over the grotesque cartoon, hollow-eyed and sunken, as if the joke itself had drained him.

A couple of college kids wearing University of Louisville cardinal red and black hoodies spotted him from the doorway, whispered too loudly, then smirked. "Hey, you do the Goatman Challenge yet?" one called after him. Their laughter followed as he crossed the next block.

By the time his parents pulled up outside Derby City Diner, Jimmy wanted nothing more than to go home. But his mother insisted. "We need a night together. Just the three of us. Normal." Her voice had that brittle edge that meant the opposite.

Inside, the neon buzzed and the air smelled of fry oil and onions. A big laminated sign hung over the specials board: "GOATMAN BURGERS! 100% beef patty topped with goat cheese and trestle truffles."

Sandra froze at the doorway, eyes locked on the sign, her lips tightening. Barry slid an arm around her shoulders, steering her gently toward the host stand. Jimmy watched them both, his stomach souring.

"Mom," he said quietly, "do you want to go somewhere else?"

Sandra shook her head hard, almost too fast. "No, no… Let's just sit down. Let's eat."

The hostess led them to a booth, vinyl seats cracked and duct-taped, and handed out menus. They hadn't been open a minute before a waitress bounced over, smile as wide as the Ohio River.

"Hi, welcome to Derby City Diner!" she chirped, pad and pen already in hand. "Would you like to try the new Goatman Burger? It's been really popular this week."

The three of them sat in silence.

"We also have another special that's not on the menu, Pope Lick Peanut Butter milkshakes. They're pretty good!"

Sandra's eyes glistened, fixed on the tabletop. Barry stiffened as he cleared his throat. Finally, he managed, "Just… give us a minute. We need to look at the menu."

The waitress lingered just a beat too long, still smiling, before retreating.

Jimmy stared at the specials board across the room, the words blaring back at him like a cruel joke. He wanted to rip the sign down, smash the neon and punch the guy behind the counter making those stupid milkshakes. Instead, he just exhaled, long and tired, and leaned back into the booth.

Sandra dabbed at her eyes with a napkin. Barry held her hand under the table. The smell of burgers and goat cheese filled the air, thick and mocking.

◆ ◆ ◆ ◆ ◆ ◆

Shelley sat slouched on the couch, the glow of the television painting her tired face in pale blues and whites. On screen, Trey Robertson's voice carried a polished cheer that didn't match the grim knot in her stomach.

"With all the hoopla surrounding the murders in the area," he said, smiling neatly into the camera, "Goatman fever has officially swept Louisville."

The broadcast cut to a quick-fire montage, a carnival of absurdity.

First: a shaky phone video beneath the Pope Lick trestle. A cluster of teenagers egged each other on, voices cracking with adrenaline. One, in a bright red Cardinals sweatshirt, threw down his backpack with mock ceremony. *Goatman Challenge, baby! First one to touch the rails wins!* He sprinted forward, only to stumble back shrieking when a deer burst from the undergrowth. The whole group scattered, their laughter dissolving into panicked screams.

Next: a corner diner. Two old men hunched over steaming plates of grits, their argument as worn as the Formica counter between them.

"I told ya, Goatman's real," the first insisted, stabbing his fork into the air. "Saw him back in '92, behind a grain silo over at the Head's farm near the creek. That thing was massive. Had to be seven foot. Big ol' horns."

His friend snorted. "You saw a damn feral dog with mange, Carl. Did you have your glasses on?"

The first guy slammed his fork down on the table, offended. "I know what I saw!"

The waitress, unimpressed, refilled their mugs without so much as a glance.

Finally: a roadside gift shop. A rack of Goatman T-shirts hung beneath postcards and novelty Bigfoot mugs. Two sunburned tourists tugged cheap goat masks over their faces, giggling like children. "If I disappear," one said, posing for a selfie, "make sure they spell my name right in the documentary."

The montage ended with a splash of graphics and a jaunty jingle.

Shelley exhaled sharply, disgusted. With a flick of her thumb, the TV screen went black. The room fell silent,

save for the faint hum of the refrigerator across the room.
She sat there a long moment, staring at her own reflection
in the dark glass, wishing—just for once—that the world
would take this nightmare seriously.

A Hive of Chaos

The hotel air conditioner hummed with a dull, mechanical wheeze, drowning the silence in its endless cycle. The bathroom door creaked open, and Priscilla emerged in a hot pink bathrobe, her beard freshly dyed jet black. It gleamed faintly under the cheap vanity bulbs, sharp and intentional, like armor.

At the mirror, Willie stood in nothing but sagging tighty-whiteys, spraying a cloud of cheap cologne across his tanned chest and pale armpits. On the bed lay the morning paper. Bold letters shouted up at him: **POPE LICK GOATMAN TRIAL BEGINS TODAY.**

He hummed tunelessly, maybe to keep the air light, maybe to drown out the headline. Sliding into a powder-blue suit that didn't quite fit—too much shoulder, too little sleeve. He fussed with the fabric as though he could will it to fit properly.

"You okay, Pris?" he asked without looking at her.

She didn't answer at first. At the sink, she dabbed at the corners of her eyes with a tissue, smearing the faintest traces of black dye onto its crumpled edges. When she finally spoke, her smile was brittle. "Yeah. I just want to look like myself when he sees me."

Willie turned toward her, his tie crooked in the mirror. "You always look like you."

She slipped out of the robe with practiced resolve, the fabric pooling at her feet. A vintage floral dress slid over her shoulders, each motion mechanical, as though dressing herself in memory more than fabric.

Willie buttoned his jacket, watching her quietly. "This ain't your fault, honey."

Her throat worked as she swallowed. She didn't argue. She didn't agree.

He crossed to the door and held it open. "You ready?"

Priscilla gathered her purse and leaned toward the bathroom counter. It was cluttered with travel debris—plastic cups, a half-empty hairspray can, the hotel's rough bar of soap. She picked up a compact mirror and a disposable razor, slipped them into her bag, and then straightened. Her lips were painted red, her eyes dry, her head high.

"Let's go see our boy."

Willie nodded, and together they stepped into the hallway. The door closed behind them with a quiet, final click.

♦ ♦ ♦ ♦ ♦ ♦

The metal cave rumbled. It was loud. A deep growl from below, a high wail from outside. Above, a constant, angry thumping beat the air. *Thump-thump-thump.* Matthew huddled on the hard bench, the rough orange fabric itching his skin. He was scared, confused. The roar of a great crowd pressed in from all sides, a terrifying wave of noise he didn't understand.

Two armed guards sat beside him. They held black sticks that smelled of cold metal. He had seen sticks like these before. They made a loud crack. They brought pain. The men's mouths moved, making sounds. The sounds were lazy, bored. One shook his head. "I can't believe Kentucky lost to Vandy. Pathetic." The other grunted. "Wait'll 'Bama hangs fifty on 'em next week. Another awful season. I'm telling you, that damn defensive coordinator has to go."

One of the men saw him watching. "Look, that got his attention," he said, nudging his partner.

The other guard chuckled. "Wonder if he's an Alabama fan."

"Nah, all that hair, he looks too much like a damn Kentucky Wildcat," the first one shot back. They both laughed.

Their laughter felt like short, sharp barks — stones being thrown at him. They were making fun of him. He knew that sound. It was the sound people made before they were cruel.

Heat bloomed in his chest. A growl rumbled in his throat, but he swallowed it. The cold metal bit into his wrists and ankles. He could not move. He could not fight. So, he stopped looking at them. He became still. He watched. He observed. His eyes flicked from the moving mouths to the black sticks, to the small, barred window where the light flashed, and then to the shiny things that dangled from one man's belt. *Keys.* He remembered keys. They opened traps.

The angry roar from outside grew louder. The metal cave slowed. He could smell it, even through the stink of the city — a faint scent of rain and wet leaves on the wind. Home. The quiet. The green. His herd. A deep, primal need surged through him: escape the noise, escape the trap. Get home.

◆ ◆ ◆ ◆ ◆ ◆

The courthouse was a hive of chaos. Trey Robertson shouted into his microphone, straining above the roar of the crowd while a cameraman fought to keep him framed. *"Good morning. We're following breaking news out of downtown Louisville where the trial of forty-three-year-old Matthew Jones — the man accused in the Pope Lick murders — is set to begin this morning. WLKL-13 has team coverage on the ground and in the air."*

Overhead, a news chopper dipped low, its camera locked onto the armored police vehicle crawling through downtown streets. Sirens wailed in the distance, echoing between glass towers.

On the ground, crowds swelled against metal barricades, voices clashing in chants and jeers. Signs bobbed above heads:

EXECUTE THE MONSTER.
HE'S STILL HUMAN.
JUSTICE FOR MORALES.
SAVE MATTHEW JONES.

Mounted police pressed through the throng, horses skittish under the noise.

A reporter near the courthouse pressed forward with her cameraman, shouting into her live feed until a trooper blocked her path. *"Ma'am, step back now — for your safety."* She retreated reluctantly, the lens still rolling.

The armored vehicle wailed through the mob, flanked by state police cruisers. Inside, Matthew Jones sat in his ill-fitting orange jumpsuit, the thick black hair spilling over his face. His eyes flicked toward the barred window, then to the jangling keys at the guard's hip. He said nothing. His silence was heavier than any words.

On the courthouse steps, Chief Hodges stood rigid with District Attorney Lester Lee and a wall of federal marshals. Their eyes scanned the crowd, reading every twitch and outburst as the sirens grew louder.

Protesters screamed at each other from either side of the barricade until a shove tipped the balance. A fist flew. The crowd buckled into violence. Officers surged to contain it. Hodges' voice cut through the bedlam like a whip: *"Keep 'em separated! Push them back!"*

Barry and Sandra Summers wove through the madness, Jimmy trailing close behind in his pressed shirt. He paused halfway up the courthouse steps, scanning the mob, and raised his phone. A swipe, and he was live, broadcasting to YouTube with shaking hands. In an instant, 1,343 views.

Across the sidewalk, Shelley stood apart from the crowd. She caught Jimmy's eye, winked, and gave him a small, steady smile. Jimmy grinned in return, bashful, before tucking his phone away.

A black government SUV rolled to the curb. Officers opened the door, and Priscilla stepped out with a handkerchief clutched tight. Her beard caught the morning light, her eyes red and wet. Willie followed, lips pressed thin. Abe rose slowly from the back seat, his tall frame unfolding with an air of quiet dread.

The noise surged. *"He's a murderer! Hang him!"* someone roared. Another voice fought back, *"He's a victim! He's been through enough!"*

The clash tipped again into shoving and screams. Riot police surged into the melee. Sirens blared.

And at the curb, framed by chaos, Priscilla stood terrified, her hand instinctively grabbing for Willie's. Her mouth opened as if to speak, but no words came. She looked desperately toward Abe, only to find him as stunned as she was, caught between the howling crowd and the courthouse doors.

Thirty yards away, almost lost in the middle of the hysteria, the armored vehicle ground to a halt. The rear doors swung open, and Matthew Jones—the Monster—was hauled into daylight, wrists and ankles shackled. His shaggy hair hung over his face, his orange jumpsuit straining against his massive frame.

He stumbled as his bare feet hit the pavement. Then, with startling speed, he drove his shoulder into the guard nearest him, slamming the man against the steel side of the truck. The clatter of metal followed—keys tumbling to the ground.

In one violent motion, Matthew snapped the chain of his cuffs, scooped the keys, twisted them into the lock, and yanked himself free. He tore at the ankle restraints, cast them off, and dropped low, weight shifting.

The guards shouted-*"Hey! HEY!"* as guns rose from all sides. But the crowd was too dense. No one had a clean shot.

Then he bolted.

An orange and black blur of muscle and matted hair, he bounded on all fours into the sea of people. Protestors screamed, scattering. Reporters toppled over tripods and cords as the mass collapsed in panic. Bodies were flung aside as he plowed through them, hurling men like rag dolls, using sheer size and speed to carve a path toward the street.

Hodges froze, staring in disbelief as Matthew tore free from the chaos and vanished down the avenue.

"Shut down the perimeter!" he roared, snapping out of it. "Block every street! I want a manhunt—NOW!"

Abe stepped forward, Shelley at his side, his voice cutting across the panic. "Wait... wait! He's not trying to hurt anyone!"

Hodges' brow wrinkled as he waved him off, already barking orders to his men, his face carved from panic and fury.

Out on the street, the creature ran free. Shackles clattered as he tore forward, his orange jumpsuit hanging off his massive, hairy frame. Sirens wailed from every direction.

A police cruiser skidded across the pavement, blocking his path. For a brief moment it seemed he might be trapped — then he launched himself into the air, landing with a bone-jarring thud on the windshield. The police officer inside gasped as the glass spider-webbed beneath hairy feet. In a blur, the creature sprinted across the roof and vaulted off the trunk, hitting the pavement in a crouch before disappearing down a narrow side street.

The officer tumbled out of the car, gun drawn, staring after him in shock.

Matthew was already gone.

He tore through a crowded lot of food trucks, tables crashing, tacos and sodas cans exploding into the air as people screamed and scattered. He didn't slow, vaulting a fence in a single bound and dropping into an alley, his movements as fluid as an animal in its natural terrain. With a guttural snarl, he hooked his fingers into the collar of the bright orange jumpsuit and ripped the fabric from his body, casting the shredded symbol of his captivity aside. Now free, he continued his desperate flight down the alley.

Above, the steady whir of rotors cut through the morning air. A police chopper circled the blocks, a heavily armed officer watching between rooftops and alleyways.

"Suspect heading southeast… toward the rail line," the pilot's voice crackled over the radio. "Repeat, he's heading for the woods."

Moments later, the creature broke through the treeline at Pope Lick Creek, crashing into the dense cover of the woods. Branches whipped against his skin, his breath coming ragged but relentless. He vanished into the shadows where no siren could follow.

A single patrol car screeched to a halt on the gravel shoulder. Hodges and Officer Cole leapt out, weapons drawn, eyes raking the wall of green where the fugitive had disappeared.

Cole's voice was tight, urgent. "I think I know where he's going. He's got some kind of a lair—past the creek bend, over the big boulder. That's where I found that old doll."

Chief Hodges' command cut through the radios and the echo of boots on gravel. *"Get every available unit down here. Right now!"*

An hour later, dusk had begun to sink its teeth into Pope Lick Creek. The woods bristled with movement—local police, SWAT, and state troopers fanned out in tight, disciplined lines. Yellow tape fluttered like ribbons in the breeze, marking off the perimeter. Drones whirred above the canopy, their red lights blinking like distant stars.

Chief Hodges stood at the edge of the treeline, flanked by Cole and a cluster of officers. His voice carried hard and sharp.

"He's fast. This is a containment operation. Fan out, stay sharp, and *do not fire* unless ordered. We bring him in alive."

Cole added grimly, "Watch the ground. Caves, ravines — anything dark, anything deep. He knows these woods better than we do."

From above, the scene resembled a living map—dozens of men with rifles and body armor threading their way through the trees like ants in formation.

But higher still, tucked in the dense branches, another set of eyes watched. The creature crouched silently, chest heaving, fur damp with sweat and fog. He shifted with predatory precision, invisible in the canopy until his pupils caught a scrap of dying light and flashed.

In his palm, a handful of acorns.

He flicked them into the underbrush with sudden force.

The clatter drew the nearest line of officers, who turned in unison and surged toward the sound, radios chirping, boots pounding. The creature remained motionless, crouched, his head tilted like a hunter gauging his prey. His breath slowed, patient.

Fog began to drift thicker through the trunks as night pulled in. Radios hissed static.

"Fan out! Watch the trestle!" Hodges bellowed, his voice muffled by the low mist.

Above them, a helicopter thundered, its spotlight carving frantic arcs through the trees and over the trestle's steel spine.

Cole drew closer to Hodges, his words clipped but certain. "If he's heading anywhere, it'll be back to that cave."

Hodges nodded once, resolute. "Then that's where we're going."

Cole motioned for two SWAT officers and disappeared into the fog, his boots vanishing into the murk. Hodges followed a moment later, the woods closing in behind them.

Manhunt

From the thicket, Matthew crept forward on all fours, his breath steady, controlled. He moved with an animal's patience, every step deliberate, every pause calculated.

At a shallow creek, he stopped. Lowering his face to the water, he drank in long, careful pulls, ripples spreading outward in silence.

On the far bank, a dozen wild goats grazed among the roots of a toppled tree. Their heads lifted as he emerged, but they did not flee. Instead, they parted just enough to make room, as though acknowledging him.

He slipped into their midst without fear. A white goat nudged him gently, curious. Another bleated softly before pressing its head to his side, trusting. Matthew lowered himself into the dirt and began to pluck burrs and twigs from their coats with a slow, practiced hand. His touch was gentle, almost tender.

A smaller goat nosed against his shoulder. He brushed debris from its eyes and exhaled a low sound, half hum, half sigh— soothing, calming.

The flock circled loosely around him, their movements unhurried, grazing in a kind of orbit. In that clearing, he was not apart from them. He was one of them. Or perhaps something more.

Then—above the trees—the faint thrum of a helicopter.

Matthew froze, ears tilting toward the sound. The goats froze with him, heads raised, as though they too understood the danger.

Slowly, he stood. The herd pressed in close,

brushing against his sides, their bodies a living wall of protection. He turned his face skyward, nostrils flaring, listening to the dull chop of blades cutting through the air.

Without hurry, he moved back into the shadows of the woods, and the goats followed — slipping after him like a flock guided by something older than instinct.

In moments, they were gone. The woods fell still again, as if nothing had stirred there at all.

Jimmy slipped through the trees, glancing over his shoulder every few steps to make sure none of the authorities had seen them slip into the park.

A soft rain began to fall, drops threading through the canopy. Suddenly- footsteps behind him. His heart raced.

Shelley.

A sigh of relief.

She stepped closer, her hair dampening in the mist.

"Thought you might do something stupid," she said, her voice steady despite the nerves underneath. "Figured I'd tag along." She gave a small shrug. "Didn't think to bring my umbrella..."

Their eyes met — an unspoken acknowledgment of the danger — and then they pushed into the trees together.

Jimmy whispered, almost giddy with nerves, "I'm going live."

He ducked behind a tree line, raising his phone. The viewer count shot from one to four thousand six hundred in seconds, climbing fast. His eyes widened. He nudged Shelley, holding the screen out to her. "Look at this."

The woods seemed alive with sound: the baying of hounds, the clipped calls of officers, radios crackling through the drizzle. Jimmy and Shelley moved carefully, weaving around trees and stones.

A sudden rustle caught Jimmy's attention. A goat darted past them, slipping between the trees with uncanny speed. He pointed, heart hammering. "Look!"

They followed, slipping deeper into the green.

♦ ♦ ♦ ♦ ♦ ♦

The woods were cordoned off with yellow crime-scene tape, stretched tight between the trees and glowing under the stutter of blue police lights. A line of patrol cars boxed in the clearing, their engines humming while a restless crowd pressed at the perimeter.

Priscilla, Willie, and Abe pushed their way to the front, their faces strained with urgency. Priscilla lunged toward the tape at once, her scarf sliding askew, but an officer moved to intercept, lifting a steady hand.

"Ma'am, I'm sorry," he said gently. "You can't go in there. It's dangerous."

Priscilla scoffed, wild panic flashing in her eyes. "My baby is out there! You have to let me through Please!"

Another officer stepped forward, this one sterner, his tone sharp as he cast a glance over the crowd. "No one is getting through. Go home, ma'am." He raised his voice so it carried to the others pressing close. "Show's over! Everyone needs to leave!"

Priscilla bent low, trying to duck beneath the tape, but the officer's hard stare froze her in place. She stepped back, trembling. Abe laid a steadying hand on her shoulder.

"Priscilla," he murmured, "they're not going to let us through. We don't want to get arrested. We should go."

Willie stepped up beside them, his shoulders squared, frustration tightening his features. "We're not leaving," he said firmly. "We'll find someone to talk to."

Abe looked between them, then back at the unflinching police line. His shoulders sagged with quiet defeat. Shaking his head, he stepped away from the tape.

Priscilla's voice rose behind him, fierce and unrelenting. "Who is the commanding officer here?! I need to speak to the person in charge!"

Abe's shoulders sagged. He looked once more at the wall of uniforms and tape, then shook his head. Turning away, he walked slowly into the crowd. His cane pressed into the grass, leaving no sound as he slipped from sight.

By the time Priscilla's voice rose again — fierce and demanding, Abe was already gone, making his way back home.

Officer Cole walked beside Captain Dunn as the woods grew darker around them, the canopy strangling out what little daylight remained. The silence of the forest was a heavy, pressing thing; even the insects seemed to be holding their breath. He pointed ahead, toward a jagged rise of limestone where brush clung to the rock like a veil.

"That's it," Cole whispered, his voice tight. "The cave. That's where Stark and Morales were killed. Not much light inside. If he's here, he'll be waiting."

Dunn raised a fist and the column of men stilled. Their rifles gleamed faintly in the dark, every man tense, breaths shallow in the quiet. One by one they moved closer, boots pressing softly into the damp earth. Cole's chest tightened with each step, the air growing thick with the smell of wet rot and something else, something musky and feral.

The brush gave way under Dunn's hand, revealing a black opening in the stone—a narrow, silent mouth that seemed to exhale cold, metallic air. Without a word, the men slipped inside.

The air turned damp, reeking of mold and iron. Roots hung from the ceiling like veins, dripping slow rivulets of water. Dunn swept his flashlight beam across the crude walls when the light snagged on something unexpected—a cracked funhouse mirror propped against the stone. A grotesque figure, hunched and massive, lunged from the glass.

He whipped his rifle to his shoulder, his finger tightening on the trigger, before he froze, realizing the warped monster in the reflection was his own. Cursing under his breath, he lowered the weapon. Their lights danced away from the mirror and across the rest of the den, revealing walls gouged out of dirt and stone

A smear of dried blood darkened the cave floor. Cole's stomach turned. He reached down, fingers brushing something brittle and wrong. When he lifted it, the bone was light in his hand, the upper half of a goat's skull, its empty sockets staring back at him like a grim warning.

"Nothing here," he muttered, though his voice betrayed the unease in his throat. He had expected to find the creature crouched in the shadows, waiting. The absence was worse, a void that made the cave feel alive, as though something had already slipped past them, unseen.

Cole rose slowly, his jaw tight, his light still sweeping the empty corners. The men shuffled behind him, their weapons finding no target in the darkness. Matthew wasn't there.

A hot wave of frustration washed over Cole, overriding the cold fear. He had come back to this place, to the spot where his friends had died, expecting a fight, an end. The emptiness felt like an insult. He kicked a loose rock, sending it skittering into the shadows. "Damnit," he hissed under his breath.

The Trestle

In the woods, the trestle loomed ahead like a giant's skeleton. Jimmy breath caught as he stopped suddenly. Shelley followed his gaze.

Through the trees, they saw him.

Matthew. Moving slowly, deliberate, surrounded by a dozen goats that followed as though tethered to his will.

Jimmy's phone trembled in his hand. The number of viewers leapt—sixteen thousand, then seventeen, climbing with every heartbeat. "It's like he's leading them out of here," he whispered.

Shelley's eyes were fixed on the strange procession. "Looks like it."

A sharp bleat broke the silence. One goat had noticed them. The others turned, restless. Matthew paused.

Then he turned.

Time froze. He began to move toward them, his massive frame slipping between the trees with an unnerving grace.

Jimmy's phone quivered in his grip—thirty-three thousand watching. Shelley's fingers fumbled through her pockets. No pepper spray. "What do we do?" she whispered.

Jimmy couldn't answer. His throat locked.

The Goatman stepped right up to him, towering, shaggy hair dripping with rain.

Jimmy froze, still holding his phone. Sixty-four thousand viewers and climbing.

Mathew swatted the phone aside, sending it into

the mud, then leaned close enough for Jimmy to feel his breath. His nostrils flared as he sniffed, low and guttural.

Jimmy staggered back, panic seizing him. The creature's eyes narrowed. Recognition flickered.

He let out a low, furious bleat that rattled Jimmy's chest.

Shelley acted without thinking. She dug into her coat pocket, fingers closing around the half-crushed pack of M&Ms her grandfather had given her. She tore it open, poured a few into her palm, and held them out.

"Matthew..." she whispered.

The creature froze. His eyes fell to the bright candies in her hand. Slowly, almost childlike, he plucked an orange one and rolled it between his fingers.

Then—police radios crackled through the trees.

Matthew's head snapped toward the sound. In an instant he was gone, bolting through the woods toward the trestle, the goats scattering in his wake.

Shelley and Jimmy stood frozen, hearts pounding. Then Jimmy scrambled to snatch up his phone from the mud, shoving it into his pocket.

The radios got closer, louder.

"We've got him cornered, north ridge near the creek!"

Cole burst through the brush with two officers, weapon raised. His eyes flicked to Jimmy and Shelley. "You two okay?"

Jimmy nodded, still breathless.

Cole didn't wait for more. He waved his men forward and sprinted toward the sounds of pursuit.

"Wait!" Shelley called after him, but he was already gone.

They bolted in the opposite direction, slipping back

into the trees as the chaos swelled around them. Shouts echoed, the clatter of boots rising above the storm.

The officers burst through a clearing, rain plastering their uniforms as they chased Matthew across the mud. Radios crackled, voices barked—some arguing whether to take a shot, others reminding them of Hodges' order: no kill shots. Not unless there was no other choice.

Matthew sprinted ahead, wild and frantic, his body a black blur against the gray curtain of rain. He climbed a rise with staggering speed, slipping and clawing his way up through the muck. At the top of the hill, he collapsed into a patch of tall grass, his chest heaving, trying to disappear into the earth itself.

All around him, the net drew tighter—boots sloshing in the mud, rifles raised, snipers waiting above the ridge.

Fighting their way up the hill in the rain, two figures in ghillie suits crawled into position, their movements slow and reptilian. Through high-powered scopes, they watched the patch of grass where the creature lay panting. The rain beaded on their rifle barrels. The chatter in Hodges' earpiece was a calm, professional counterpoint to the storm.

"Alpha-One is in position. We have a clean visual."

Another voice, Captain Dunn's, cut in. "All teams, hold the perimeter."

Hodges stood near the edge of the trestle, rain dripping from the brim of his hat. He sized up the situation. The trestle was a long, open bottleneck. If Matthew bolted, he'd be gone. He raised the radio to his mouth.

"Dunn, I need a team to circle around to the far side of the trestle. I want him surrounded in case he makes a run for it."

A voice crackled back in his earpiece. "Yes, sir. Need a few minutes to get over there and into position."

Hodges lowered the radio, his eyes still locked on the figure huddled at the far end. He knew it was going to take a few precious minutes to get them in position. Minutes they might not have.

"Chief, this is Alpha-One," the sniper's voice crackled again, impossibly calm. "Target is exposed. I have the shot. Awaiting your command."

Hodges squeezed his radio, the plastic groaning under the pressure. He had to bring him in alive. He owed the boy that much.

"All units hold!" he barked, his voice cutting through the chaos. "I want him contained, not dead!"

Jimmy and Shelley pushed through the police line, rain soaking their hair and clothes. Jimmy's voice cracked as he called out.

"Chief, don't shoot him! He's just scared!"

Hodges didn't look away from the sight of Matthew trembling at the far end. "Son, that thing is a cornered predator. Get back before you get hurt."

He cupped a hand to his mouth and shouted into the storm. "It's okay, Matthew! We just want to help!"

But Matthew answered with a guttural bleat, the sound raw with terror. He scrambled backward onto the slick ties of the trestle, every inch of him screaming to escape.

Jimmy's stomach knotted. He could see the snipers adjusting their aim. Time was running out. He pulled out his phone and turned to Shelley.

"They're going to kill him."

He tapped the screen. The red livestream icon

blinked alive. Shoving past a startled Officer Cole, Jimmy stepped onto the trestle, phone held high like a fragile shield.

"Kid, no!" Cole shouted. "Get back here!"

But Jimmy ignored him. He walked steadily and slow down the center of the track, the rain slick beneath his shoes. The livestream number jumped instantly: 45,520 viewers.

"They're going to kill him," Jimmy told the camera, voice breaking. "He's not a monster. His name is Matthew Jones..."

Viewers skyrocketed—70,011, then climbing faster. The officers faltered, unsure now with a boy in their line of fire.

Jimmy stopped twenty feet from the creature. Lowering his phone, he kept it recording but fixed his eyes on Matthew. The counter surged—102,368.

"Matthew," Jimmy whispered, softer now. "Matty Matty..."

Matthew growled low, his filthy hands gripping the wood so tight his knuckles blanched. His muscles trembled, ready to spring.

From behind, Shelley's voice rang out. "Jimmy, the M&Ms!"

She pulled the half-empty bag from her pocket and tossed it underhanded. The little bag skittered across the wet ties, sliding to a stop at Jimmy's feet.

Jimmy crouched slowly, heart hammering, and picked it up. His hand shook as he poured a few candies into his palm, holding them out like an offering.

"You remember these, don't you?"

For a heartbeat, the storm stilled. Matthew's wild eyes softened, the growl dying in his throat. His head tilted, the faintest trace of memory flickering in his face.

Hodges stiffened. Every officer looked to him, waiting.

Then, with a trembling step, Matthew reached forward. His hand extended, almost touching the boy.

BOOM!

A gunshot tore the moment apart. A rookie officer on the flank panicked, his rifle bucking. The bullet screamed past, striking the steel rail beside Matthew with a shrieking ping that echoed into the rain.

Matthew flinched, shrieked in terror, and stumbled backward. His feet slipped on the trestle's slick timbers. For the briefest instant, his eyes locked with Jimmy's—filled with shock, fear, and something achingly human.

Then he was gone.

He plunged into the rushing dark below, swallowed by the violent creek.

Jimmy stood frozen, his hand still outstretched, the rain running down his face like tears. Officers rushed past, their boots hammering the soaked wood.

"What the..." Cole breathed, stunned.

Chief Hodges raised the radio to his mouth, his voice heavy with defeat. "Get eyes on the water! He's down! Start recovery! Everyone to the creek! I repeat, everyone to the creek!"

As Hodges's orders crackled over the radios, the two SWAT team members who had just gotten into position on the far side of the trestle rushed toward the center. They reached Jimmy, their black tactical gear slick with rain. One of them placed a firm hand on his shoulder.

"You okay, kid?" the officer asked, his voice muffled slightly by his gear.

Jimmy didn't seem to hear him at first, his eyes still fixed on the churning black water below. The officer gave his shoulder a gentle shake. "Kid?"

Finally, Jimmy pulled his eyes away from the creek and looked at the officer, his expression vacant. He gave a slow, numb nod.

◆ ◆ ◆ ◆ ◆ ◆

Rain sheeted down as flashlights slashed through the dark. Helicopters thundered overhead, their beams cutting across the swollen creek. Boats drifted back and forth below, spotlights raking the surface. Dogs barked. Search teams shouted into the night.

On the jagged rocks beneath the trestle, an officer crouched low, calling sharp into his radio.

"Chief, you've got to see this."

His light revealed it: a dark, wet smear of blood staining the stone, strands of coarse, matted hair clinging to the rock.

"He must've hit his head before he ever went into the water," the officer continued. "No one could survive that, sir. The current must've taken the body."

From the bank above, Chief Hodges stood rigid, staring at the rolling black water. His shoulders sagged. His head lowered.

"Damn it..." he murmured.

A news crew crept closer, their camera glaring in the rain as the reporter whispered to her mic. Hodges caught sight of them and snapped to Cole.

"Damnit, get them out of here."

Cole moved fast, stepping into their light. "Not now," he barked, shoving the lens aside. "Please — get back."

The reporter pressed, trying to push past, but Cole's presence loomed large, unyielding, until they finally retreated into the crowd of flashing lights and rain.

♦ ♦ ♦ ♦ ♦ ♦

Later that night, Abe sat on the edge of his bed, the television screen painting his face in cold, flickering light. The footage looped again and again—crowds surging outside the courthouse, police pressed against barricades, the armored transport swallowed by chaos. He watched with heavy stillness, the weight of the day pressing down on him until it was hard to breathe.

The broadcast cut sharply, Trey Robertson standing in the rain by the darkened banks of Pope Lick Creek. Police tape snapped in the wind behind him, officers pacing the shadows like restless sentinels. Trey's voice was grave, carrying words Abe had dreaded since the manhunt began.

"Authorities have confirmed that the so-called 'Goatman' was killed last night during a manhunt near Pope Lick Creek."

The scene shifted to District Attorney Lester Lee at an impromptu press conference in his office, his face drawn, shoulders bowed under exhaustion. Cameras flashed like lightning.

"No body has been recovered at this time," Lee said, his voice low. "But given the amount of blood at the scene, and the height of the fall—I don't believe anyone could have survived it." He hesitated, eyes down, and when he spoke again there was sorrow threaded through the gravel of his voice. "I wanted to bring him in. Let him have his day in court. But things happened fast. Too fast."

The broadcast returned to the newsroom. Footage played in the corner of the screen: boats combing the river, officers dragging nets across the current, helicopters sweeping harsh white beams through the black water. The anchor's polished tone carried a note of finality.

"It looks like the Pope Lick Goatman saga has finally come to a close. The man at the center of this bizarre case, Matthew Jones—had become not just a local fascination, but his story has piqued people's interest nationwide. However, tonight, it appears his tragic story has ended."

Abe's throat tightened. He tried to swallow against it, but the grief was too much. Tears welled and spilled before he could stop them, streaking down his broad cheeks. He dragged the back of his hand across his face, as if angry at himself for letting it show, but the tears kept coming.

Alone in the dim room, with only the drone of the newscast for company, Abe bowed his head. His chest shuddered, his body trembling with the force of loss he couldn't put into words. Matthew was gone. And with him, a piece of Abe's heart had been carried into the dark water of the creek.

Just then, the sharp ring of his cell phone cut through the silent room, making him jolt. He fumbled for it on the nightstand, his large hands still trembling. He answered, his voice a rough croak.

"Hello?"

He listened for a moment to the urgent voice on the other end.

"Yes," he said, his voice heavy with grief. "I'm watching it now…"

Beloved Son

Two days later, the small chapel at Meadow View Funeral Home was quiet. At the front rested a modest casket, closed, with a small brass plaque affixed to its top:

MATTHEW JONES – Beloved Son

Rows of metal folding chairs sat nearly empty. At the back, a handful of local reporters scribbled in notebooks, their cameras resting on their laps. *Vultures*, Willie thought, aggravated they couldn't just let it be.

He sat stiff-backed and stone-faced in the front row, forcing himself to stare straight ahead. Beside him, Priscilla's hand trembled as she clutched a damp, crumpled tissue. Abe, seated between them, had his hands clasped tight in his lap, his massive shoulders slumped in a convincing portrait of sorrow.

Near the entrance, on a small wooden table, sat a modest bouquet of flowers. Abe's eyes fell on the small white card tucked inside. He walked over and read the messy script: "Sorry for your loss. Your friends at Sterling Stetson's Used Cars." A sound escaped Abe's lips—a dry, humorless half-chuckle. From the front row, Willie spotted him.

"Yeah," Willie muttered, shaking his head slightly. "Ain't that something..."

The priest's voice filled the stillness, steady but gentle. "We are here not to bury the creature from the headlines," he said, "but to finally lay to rest Matthew Jones. A beloved son, lost to the world for forty years... Today, we return him to the loving arms of his family, and to the eternal peace of God, where all suffering ends."

Priscilla dabbed at her cheeks, her tissue dissolving in her grip. Willie remained rigid, unmoving, his eyes dark and fixed on the casket. Abe lowered his head, blinking fast, fighting to breathe evenly.

When the priest finished, he gave a small, respectful bow before slipping quietly toward the side door. Willie nodded faintly, his jaw tightening as if in gratitude he could not voice.

At the rear of the room, the reporters began to file out, sensing the story was over. All but one. Trey Robertson lingered in a back pew, closing his notebook but keeping his eyes on the scene, observing. He watched as Chief Hodges entered, his uniform pressed, his face drawn with fatigue. The priest murmured a greeting, "Hello, Chief." Hodges forced a smile before stepping forward.

"Mr. and Mrs. Jones," he said quietly, his voice heavy, "I'm so sorry for your loss." He paused, searching for words that wouldn't come. "I wish I had the words."

Priscilla swallowed hard. Her lips trembled as though she might refuse him, but she steadied herself, smoothing the crumpled tissue in her hand. "Thank you for coming," she managed, her voice thin but kind. "I know this isn't pleasant. I know it isn't the part of your job you signed up for."

"Yes, ma'am," Hodges replied with a solemn nod. His eyes lingered a moment, full of something almost tender. "I genuinely am sorry all this happened."

For the first time that day, Willie's hardened expression softened. Hodges shifted his eyes to Abe, offering a small, weary smile.

"Abe," he said quietly, "come by the office sometime. We can go grab lunch."

Abe nodded, the gesture slow but sincere. Hodges gave them one last look, then turned and stepped away.

Seeing the chief leave, Trey Robertson finally stood. He gave Priscilla a brief, practiced smile of condolence and then slipped out the door, the story finally, truly over.

The heavy chapel door clicked shut, leaving the three of them in total silence. In the quiet that followed, Abe shared a heavy, unspoken moment with Willie and Priscilla.

◆ ◆ ◆ ◆ ◆

On the other side of town, Jimmy's room glowed in the soft ring of artificial light, the halo making his tired face look older than his years. He sat at his desk, shoulders slouched, eyes steady on the phone balanced in its tripod. His voice was quieter, almost reverent, as if he were talking to a single person rather than thousands.

"Hey everyone," he began. "Jimmy Summers here. This isn't my usual kind of video, but I just wanted to talk... really talk."

He paused, swallowing hard. "These past few days have been hell. I lost my brother, my uncle... and for a while, I thought maybe I was losing my mind too."

His reflection stared back at him through the lens, glassy-eyed but unflinching. "There was a time I wanted to see the monster suffer for what he did to my family. And somewhere along the way, I got lost. I started watching the subscriber numbers climb... and a part of me liked it. And I feel sick about that. Because it was never supposed to be about the numbers. It was supposed to be about my brother."

The words hung in the quiet room. He leaned closer to the camera, voice low, almost confessional.

"A lot of people have been asking me a question since they found out who the Goatman really was. They ask if I can forgive him. If I can forgive the man who killed my brother and my uncle. And the honest answer is... no. I don't think I can. I don't know if I'll ever be able to forgive that. What he took from me... from my family... you can't get that back."

He drew a shaky breath.

"But I've learned something else. I learned that you don't have to forgive to understand. And I understand now. I understand that the thing that took my brother wasn't an evil monster. It was a scared little boy, lost in the woods forty years ago, who grew up into a man who was just... surviving."

His voice softened, almost a whisper. "Now... I think I just want peace. For my family. For Matthew Jones' family. The views don't matter. What matters is how we heal."

A small smile tugged at his lips. "So, this will be the last J. Summertime video for a while. I need to just be Jimmy. But I wanted to say thank you to everyone who reached out. And even though I lost a lot... I did gain something."

At that, Shelley drifted into frame, gentle and sure, sliding an arm around his shoulder. He leaned into her without hesitation.

"He means someone," she teased softly, smiling at the camera.

Jimmy blushed, laughing under his breath. Their eyes met — genuine, warm, fragile but steady. "Life is getting better," he said.

The door creaked open behind them. Jimmy startled slightly, turning to see Sandra framed in the light of the hallway. Her voice was plain, motherly. "You know it's a school night. Have you got your homework done?"

Shelley giggled. Jimmy gave a sheepish grin. "Yes, ma'am. Well, kinda…"

He reached forward, thumb brushing the screen, and ended the recording. "I'll get right on it…"

Southbound

The Greyhound bus hummed steadily down I-65, its headlights cutting through the dusk as the sky bled into burnt orange over flat fields and distant tree lines. Inside, the air was thick with the low murmur of passengers and the rhythmic hiss of tires against asphalt.

Willie sprawled across two seats near the middle, his tropical button-down mostly unbuttoned, chest rising and falling in heavy sleep. His mouth hung open, soft snores rattling, while a battered copy of *Men's Health* lay forgotten on his chest.

A row behind him, Priscilla sat upright in the aisle seat, a portrait of composed eccentricity. Oversized sunglasses concealed her eyes, her bright pink blouse crisp against the bus's worn upholstery. Her beard, freshly dyed, shimmered faintly under the harsh fluorescent lights, though her smile — fixed, tight — looked more like armor than joy.

Beside her sat a man, clean-shaven, pale, his bald head wrapped with a heavy bandage. He stared blankly out the window, his reflection flickering against the fading light.

Priscilla shifted, her voice breaking the silence in a soft murmur.

"We'll be home soon, Matthew," she whispered. "You're safe with Momma."

The man turned. His eyes — dark, haunted — met hers. His teeth, crooked and rotting, broke through a faint, almost childlike smile. Despite the neat clothes, despite the attempt at disguise, there was no mistaking him. Matthew Jones.

Cradled against his chest was a brand-new Raggedy Andy doll, its red yarn hair spilling between his fingers. He clutched it tightly, as though it might anchor him to this new, fragile version of life.

Priscilla leaned close, kissing his cheek with quiet tenderness, the gesture at once maternal and defiant.

The bus rumbled onward, carrying them into the glowing dusk until the machine itself became only a shadow rolling toward the southern horizon.

Downstream

FLASHBACK

After Matthew fell from the trestle, Chief Hodges stood on the bank, in the rain, watching the spotlights from the search boats cut uselessly through the black, churning water. Every officer was following his orders, combing the area around the trestle. But a gut feeling, the kind that had kept him alive for forty years, gnawed at him. There was a small cove a quarter-mile downstream, choked with driftwood and debris, that the boats couldn't easily reach. He had told no one; he just walked away from the lights and followed the rushing sound of the creek into the darkness.

He found him there. Matthew was tangled in a mess of fallen branches, his body broken and bleeding, but his chest was rising and falling in shallow, ragged breaths. He was alive. Barely.

Hodges's hand went to his radio. He could end it right there. Call it in. The manhunt would be over. Matthew would be taken to a prison hospital, put on trial, and become a sideshow freak all over again, this time for the whole world to see. He looked down at the unconscious man—not a monster, just a broken boy in a forty-year-old body—and thought of the note he'd written as a rookie: *Matthew Jones, Age 3, MISSING*. The ghost that had haunted his entire career.

He made his choice. He raised the radio to his mouth, his voice firm. "This is Hodges. We've found significant blood evidence on the rocks below the trestle. No way to survive a fall from that distance. This is now a recovery operation, not a rescue. Repeat, a recovery."

He clicked the radio off, severing the connection to the official world. He couldn't move Matthew alone. He took out his personal cell phone and made one call to the only person he knew would understand.

"Abe," Hodges said. "It's Hodges…"

Epilogue

Two months later, the view through the GoPro lens was shaky, catching glimpses of sun-dappled sand and twisted scrub pines.

"Alright, folks, Randy Hawkins here, coming at you from beautiful Orange Beach, Alabama," he narrated, his voice casual. "Decided to come south for the winter, get away from all that… crazy stuff up in Kentucky. Found this sweet little nature trail right behind the condo, the Rattlesnake Ridge Trail."

He panned the camera across a stretch of quiet, sun-bleached woods. "Nice and peaceful down here. So much warmer. A lot different from Pope Lick, I'll tell you that much." He chuckled, the sound a little hollow. "No spooky trestles, no… well, you know."

He paused, listening. The trail was silent. "Actually, it's real quiet. Don't even hear any birds."

He took a few more steps, the soles of his shoes scuffing against the concrete path, the camera jostling with his stride. He was about to speak again when a sound cut through the stillness. Not a bird. Not a squirrel.

A low, guttural bleat. Warped and wrong. Randy froze, the camera holding steady on the empty path ahead.

"What the…?" he whispered.

The bleat came again, closer this time. He turned abruptly…

Too late.

Snow sifted gently outside the frosted window of Abe's small room at Willow Glen, the flakes glowing against the gray December sky. Holiday decorations — cheap garlands and paper snowflakes — clung to his door, their cheer brittle and faint. Abe sat sunk in his armchair, the television muttering endlessly in the corner, filling the silence.

On screen, a reporter stood in a sun-bleached stretch of Alabama woods, the breeze stirring dry grass behind her.

"...officials here in Orange Beach are still trying to identify the remains," she said, her tone grave, "but they confirm they belong to a hiking enthusiast who went missing last week on the Rattlesnake Ridge Trail."

A gentle knock broke the moment. The door creaked open and a nurse stepped in, smiling, an envelope pinched between her fingers.

"Another Christmas card for you, Abe," she said.

He took it, nodding his thanks. The envelope was bright red, cheerful against his weathered hands. He glanced at the return address, and something in him faltered — a flicker of memory, sorrow, recognition. Carefully, almost reverently, he peeled open the seal.

Inside was a Christmas card. The front showed a tacky trailer smothered in pink flamingos and gaudy string lights. He opened it. The handwriting inside was neat, looping cursive:

Happy Holidays from your friends in Orange Beach!
— The Jones Family

Abe's mouth softened into the faintest of smiles. Friendly. Simple. But when his eyes drifted back to the television, his body stiffened.

The reporter's voice cut sharper now:

"This marks the third disappearance in Orange Beach since November..."

Abe froze. His eyes flicked from the glowing television screen to the card in his lap.

"Orange Beach?" he whispered, the word tasting strange, dangerous.

His gaze dropped again to the neat handwriting: *The Jones Family.*

His smile vanished. The warmth drained from his face. A slow, dawning horror spread through his chest as the connection locked into place.

The TV droned on, but Abe no longer heard it. He could only stare at the card trembling slightly in his hands.

If you enjoyed *Below the Trestle*, please consider leaving a review at Amazon.com.

www.ingramcontent.com/pod-product-compliance
Lightning Source LLC
Chambersburg PA
CBHW061919130726
47908CB00017B/2469